QUILT
A Collection Of Prose

QUILT
A Collection Of Prose
by
Finola Moorhead

Sybylla Co-operative Press and Publications
1985

Sybylla Press is a feminist printing and publishing co-operative established in 1976 in Melbourne.

Published by Sybylla Co-operative Press and Publications Ltd.
© Finola Moorhead, 1985
© Cover: Sybylla Co-operative Press and Publications Ltd.
No part of this work may be reproduced in any form without the written permission of the publisher.

National Library of Australia Cataloguing-in-Publication entry:
Quilt, a collection of prose
ISBN 0 908205 04 X
1. Australian prose literature — 20th century. I. Title.
A828'.308

Printed by Sybylla Co-operative Press and Publications Ltd,
193 Smith Street, Fitzroy, Australia.
Typeset in Baskerville by Abb-typesetting Pty Ltd,
Collingwood, Australia.
Cover by Lin Tobias

In memory of my mother who had faith in my literary ability and who only showed me this at the times when I most needed it.

For my friends without whose help, inspirationally, emotionally and financially, I would not have been able to continue writing as I have done.

Contents

Confession From A Ghost-White Albino Skin	6
So, Sandra	8
Clown Pieces	11
Five Finger Exercises	19
Conversation Without Inverted Commas	31
Jillian Arbus	34
Seven Abortions	45
Bloomsbury's Son	51
Moreton Bay Fig	54
Twenty-four Hours From Tulsa	57
Goodbye Prince Hamlet: The New Australian Women's Poetry	66
Sketches	74
Screams From A Primal Quarter	77
Bella	80
Prose Looks At Photographs	81
The Room With A Mirror	86
Black, Silver And Grey	91
Three Men In A Boat	93
A Nightmare Leads To A Scandal	99
Where Are You, Ellen Spalding?	104
The Rubbish Tin Outside Federation Café	113
Rooming House	115
A Book Is Launched In Soho	117

Who Cares About The Sentence? 129
Nun 132
Happening Upon A Character, In The First Person 133
A Bit Of The Learning Bit 139
Novel In Ten Lines 142
The Illusive Quality Stories 143

Appendix 158

Alice Walker wrote that she is glad she was born a woman and black in this age. I guess she is glad she is American, too, and from the Southern states. The richness of the female heritage in terms of strength, endurance and various forms of oppression is undeniable today. It has arrived at the frontal lobe of the civilisation's brain — it cannot be denied and ignored by the intelligentsia anywhere. The day and age has many thousands of women writers, and that phenomenon is absolutely essential for humankind's sense of self.

Most writing women are no longer burdened by a dozen children, backbreaking work in factories, fields and kitchens, financial dependency and the legal definition of being a chattel. We're the soft-palmed women, lumped with the historical task of recording. We are saying. A monster is lifting its many heads. In waking it may seem frightening, aggressive, justifiably angry but as it gets the hearing it requires, fear of the female could lessen as it is understood. It would be foolish to think the mysterious female has not been feared, considered monstrous, dangerous, blasphemous, obscene, etc. The feminine energy in being largely dormant has increased its force. The women writers are actually the compromisers. Being aware of the power of the unsung we are prepared to explain in male language the small parts of it we comprehend. It is silly to murder the messengers, the precursors, those with white cotton flying from their banners.

Sadly, of course, we have not been greeted with banquets and enthusiastic receptions. They have glanced at the tatty edges of our messages and discarded them. They have been blind to the originality, closed their ears with their fists and dismissed the harangues as nuisances. Most women writers have a very hard time even achieving publication. The more honest and original, the more difficult. The tough in character, the noble warriors and the intellectual giants have made it through the massed ranks of conservatism and masculine self-protective measures, usually with assistance from women in the publication game. Thus we know to some extent the magnitude of this monster — the writing-women phenomenon of our time. But even those individuals with heroic attributes have tales to tell, scars to show and clear memories of the times they nearly went under.

We have it so much easier than our mothers, grandmothers and those women who used to write in the harsher ages of man's dominance. They put up with things under which our own tender neurotic souls would crack. Fortunately, we don't have to face those trials. Our trials are more insidious. They attempt to tear us from ourselves, to attack us with reason, realities and 'protesteth-too-much' style of excuses. We are asked in kindest tones with many words over a free coffee or meal, not to be so difficult, to try to reach the common taste. Our manuscripts may have received the highest praise from a leader in the literary field, and yet that will still be accompanied by a 'but': but it's probably too emotional, but there are not enough signposts to the plot, but you're not well enough known to sell, especially such unusual work, but . . .

At a reading, our manuscripts may have brought tears to the eyes of a hundred women. We have to take encouragement from this small public and turn it into inner courage. For the woman writer doesn't need encouragement as such. She has been at her desk a million hours without encouragement.

The pressure to go on may come from the female energy which has been under-expressed for so many centuries. The sense of being driven to write is not interpreted by women writers as the destiny of genius. No contemporary woman that I know of has ever claimed this peculiar fate. She would become an object of ridicule by the simple fact that there are so many of us around, and anyway it doesn't feel right. Yet men have claimed this all the time, especially at the heights of their civilisation. Even now as well, I suspect. No, the sense of having to write, even though we are told the market is not ready, is more a feeling of cultural burden. An awareness that half, maybe most, of the truth wasn't being told by traditional fiction, that the way of these stories with their ejaculatory climaxes was unsatisfactory, that she, the individual, knew she could do better, struck a whole generation with synchronatic accuracy.

A good number of this particular generation could have been the first women in their families to have gained entrance into tertiary educational institutions. Becoming a writer is a fairly classical way of reconciling working-class backgrounds with middle-class educations.

With their insights into their parents' lifestyles and problems, they were not as likely to accept the full academic trip as were their middle and upper-class counterparts. Things to write about — insights — may also have been fired by an incomprehensible guilt as they smashed the dearly held values of their folks and the pretensions of academic standards with the common sense and plain brain power they were born with.

The recent wealth of the culture has come from this mob of women all over the world, and yet there lingers in the tail of the dying patriarchal civilisation sufficient sting for us to feel righteously sore.

The rising heap of disappointments and disregard becomes assimilated into one's self-awareness as a kind of tired scepticism. It is experienced as a personal rather than political thing, women writers often being too busy to organise into effective power blocks to much alter the publishing game. Some women have organised feminist publishing co-operatives and collectives. I commend the feminist co-operative of Sybylla Press for caring to do my first book, for trusting the value of the work. Sybylla, while being such a small concern, believes in women's work enough to take risks the bigger publishers are afraid of.

Notwithstanding all this, my mind and energies are rarely preoccupied with the problems of becoming known and the economics of print, paper and production. Writing in terms of financial expenditure, is not an expensive art form. One can continue to do it with negligible funds. The main capital needed is made of commitment and time and mental energy. Pushing the imagination to the point of exhaustion, and then the application of craft in translating something amorphous into language is an employment which makes others fairly impossible.

I am a fiction writer. Most of my adult working life has been concerned with the questions and operations of this task. And in this job, like Alice Walker, I am glad I am a woman.

The most important thing in fiction-writing is subtlety. Fiction is concerned with truth without telling the truth. And I mean passionately concerned with truth. Great writers of stories will testify to this one way or another in discussing their problems. Because it is a *problem. Because coming a close second is the concern of fabrication. The temptation to fabricate more, to nobble truth as it were in this race — race, yes, for it always has an urgency, a suspense, an event-like structure — and fabricate beyond the limits of one's own known truth is often hard to resist.*

Another facet of the problem is not to get the artifice of the two jumbled. To see truth in fabrication's place, i.e. to use the wit and skills of fabrication on the truth distorts fiction. It is seeing truth as fact or fact as truth. It is the kind of fiction-writing that can be libellous. Much as observation is necessary to the good fiction-writer, recounting facts is no substitute for the truth which is fiction's chief concern. The stuff of truth is deeper material than the damning details of a recognisable person's actions and reactions. A satisfying story enlightens us as to some aspect of the general human condition. That is why it can come from any culture and be happily read in translation or can be set in another historical era and still be appreciated as if we knew the geography in it as well as would a native of the story's place.

So it is the subtlety of this play between truth and fabrication which is the real joy of reading or writing fiction. The writer may well know on whom the story is based. It should go no further. The very need of fabrication demands invention. Within the dynamics of fiction, to fabricate is a force — an artistic force, like the tension of colour in oil painting. It is more than a matter of disguise. Mere disguise is a curtain, a product of deception, not of creativity. To imagine a story is to set out out upon a road that could lead to complete fantasy, and how far you go is how far your known truth will let you, for you cannot make up the truth. You can invent all sorts of possible truths and weird and wonderful beings to people them, but I contend that even that, if it is to be enjoyable and judged as good fiction, is based on a kind of truth, an abstract and philosophical one probably — like the fable.

The art of writing fiction is to play this fine line of tension between your known truth (what you want to say) with the structures and details of invention.

As none of us know all the truth and at best know a small part, it is even an arrogance to say there is such a thing. This is the joy, this is the subtlety, to come upon insight into the human condition as if by surprise, to strike the question mark, or to, within the dark caverns of the meaning-of-it-all, manage a bit of candle-light. So when I say the 'truth', I mean something about life that we recognise beyond the details of the fabrication.

When I started to write stories, I had no idea why or what, except that reading or seeing fiction was a way I began to understand things with enjoyment. With a thrill. There has always been a tension for me between the real world and fictional ones. From one I'd learn that, from the other this. People find me peculiar to talk to because I equally value an insight gained from fiction, with fact or analysis from a factual basis. It is simply a queer turn of mind.

Confession From A Ghost-White Albino Skin

Found in a red brick comfort station.

'I cannot settle down. I am wriggling and wriggling but I do not fit. Tears have dried and my eyes itch. It certainly does not matter what caused the tears. *My eyes are itching.* I am irritated. I am annoyed by the irritation. I know there is a deeper reason for these things than they ascribe to them. They are all-powerful. They know what I am from the outside — that is what they see. They judge — my defence can be neither the tears nor the irritation. They will cast me out, dismiss me; I do not think (although it is the alternative) that they will ever gaol me but this is exactly what they want. They have gaols finer than cobwebs and stronger than steel. These gaols fit neatly into their wallets and when they reach into their pockets to pay, they deviously bring out the gaol they have woven especially for me. If their arms are around me and gentle as dew, I will have to draw in breath after breath of emotion, explode and tear off the skin and muscle to the bone, and then the bones must be snapped apart. That way they will not gaol me. That way I will be free. But at my trial, at the horrid moment of my defence, the tribunal will say with omnipotence that I have no more right to be free than they who have so many gaols on them their eyes are protected from the itch. I will have to say my eyes are free, and the tears dried leaving the irritation. All this will mean nothing to them. They will continue their ritual with kindness, and the timepieces (hourglasses, egg-timers, metronomes, grandfather clocks, watches, the bubble-handed round official clocks on the walls) will all tick until the courtroom falls to the floor. This is what I wish for — replacement of the courtroom by a paddock of hay or an enchanted forest of cabbage gums. All this is becoming impossible. They will not see that my eyes are sorely tried by a speck. If it would make them see I would willingly make the speck a beam and start it on a flamboyant circular course emblazoned with bright flags stolen from a bullring . . . (How is it they shine their lights so bright? Why do they turn the loudspeakers up so loud? How is it the room is filled with the smells of unwashed orifices? Why do they bring the dentists in to drill the teeth just for sport? Why do they dress in starched cotton, so tightly fitting and so painful? How is it they move about tearing the nerves out of their skin with the points and corners of the gravel they mixed with the starch? Why do they drink and vomit with such glee?) I know I have only a minor itch in the eye, but I suffer so much what I see. Seeing itself is a pain, but what I see is more than pain. I take it into a ghost-white albino skin I save for the purpose (pink eyes, quivering nose, soft licking tongue and ears sensitive to the flight of a leaf) and there it grinds, and glares, and groans. Inside me a little vulnerable shellfish me is exposed to all the agony they are inflicting on themselves. How I wish to leave the court-room! They all have the choice to leave, but they will not. They stay to the final shaving of the dentists' virtuosity. I cannot leave, it is I who am on trial here. It is I who am in the dock. Two large guards prevent my escape — they stand with arms folded, lips firm and downturned, but I see their eyes slide anglewise to the arena with enjoyment as they watch the sport of drills, slowly licking their lips, as the dentists go faster and faster to the climax. And when it is finished they will start another sport, and after that another, leaving me here in the dock between dismissal and gaol. Always in this crowded room there is at least one glance upon me. Escape is impossible: I do not fit into this square . . .'

So, Sandra

So, Sandra, you've written me a fan letter: if I don't choose to care at least you say you've registered your positive reaction to my story. Instantly I'm afraid of you. You are as egocentric as I, you sat down on the strength of your emotion and ambition and wrote to a stranger. It's just beautiful to feel the spring sun drying wet hair, unbrushed, uncombed. Also moss grows between the uneven bricks pressed down instead of concrete for the yard. From one window alone, mine, the full sight of a huge fountain of wistaria tumbling with blackboy roses over the tin. Come, Sandra, have some white wine with me while we smile and frown into the sun; and what will we talk of? Not me. I've said that now, I no longer want to tell you that — the big decisions that changed my life, nor the banal circumstances in which they occurred. Let people find those when I'm dead. Let's you and I talk of Virginia Woolf, incidentally mentioning Aphra Behn and Sappho — land a moment (you like the theatre and mime?) on Moliere's mistress and the one who was his wife. Soon I will invite you to join our troupe of jugglers and masked comediennes touring the countryside in a bright confronting bus — the feminist circus — al fresco salads by creeks and little bridges. Country stands at country shows and country general stores; we pick up bargains and take gifts of cast-offs with a smile. Or steal. This is the colouring in the scarf we knit and bring the revolution. Another garden of Eden. Another noble savage on the mountain where avocados grow on trees ... You sip white wine and frown away from me, you're thinking of the tiny not so glorious achievements of your own life — but your determination says, it happened yesterday — you wonder if I would be interested. You know how you felt and at least three or four very similar things have happened to me: will I cast aside the familiar, or generously emanate empathy? Suddenly I ask, do you see auras? You answer no, but if I have an ounce of proof . . . this might be another thing which changes the world.

Living is hardly more or less the ego trip. Take the pool of the moment, the present, a whole cycle of events and organisms wound together in the seemingly haphazard pinpointing of a minute, or an hour, bound by that pinpoint; take it and see it as a simple round millpond, placid and welcoming. A child is playing by the millpond. She has discovered that she can fold paper with nail-sharp straight creases into a kite that flies like a miniature sailplane. She has been making paper aeroplanes all morning, inside the house, and has air-traffic-controlled their arrivals and departures on the couch, mourned the tragedies and repaired the aircraft, within two hours. It had been a speeded up radar screen which, mysteriously, she has been both without and within. The planes became paper, quite accidentally, when she found a pen behind the door. On her favourite — this one sits in the air like a superbly designed Danish glider and dives to its destination like an eagle, landing always belly down — she wrote a secret message. She has come to the millpond holding her delicate creation in two hands. Suddenly the purpose became clear: with all her energy she shoots the paper glider high into the air and watches its path breathlessly, and, yes, it lands almost perfectly in the centre of the pond, sending subtle ripples out circle after circle until the first circle reaches the shore, then she looks back to the piece of paper. It's limp and like a stain of rubbish but the words of her secret message dissolve and become part of the pond and the tiny ripples keep occurring. And yet, I say the pond is a moment. It has produced a disturbance which is, strangely, not chaotic. A nonsensical note thrown from somewhere outside the present, and circle by circle tries to lasso . . . a chaos. Which leads me to the persona of my clown. Who throws a handspan into the light, finger by finger finds the spot, mimicking the nothing, pulled her face around the corner, grins, twinkle in the eye, winks, strutting the parody of a learned type with a lecture. Of course it all boils down to dream and reality, which is a totally different dichotomy from illusion and truth, which is again distinct from fantasy and fact, and that again from fiction and history, and again and again from play and work and so on and on, and so on. And on. My clown beams tears of frustration, sits down and shouts, why me? I only know a little bit, but I want to entertain. I played, Red played as a child, with paper aeroplanes, and later in my life I was a student pilot flying an Auster in the sky, looked down on the earth and said, From here I can see over hills and round corners. I can see cars and trucks going from A to B, and I will return to the same 'drome. I thought at that altitude I had discovered the action simile for poetry ... St Exupéry came to mind. Comes to mind, now. Poetry is fact, he actually did that flight from Arras. My clown slumped in her spotlight, says in a petulant whine, there are no dichotomies, so there! I piloted a paper dart to the middle of my own chaos ... whatever is wrong with going around in circles?

Clown Pieces

1
If you asked me why, I'd shrug and smile. This week they complimented me for the capital *I*, and then began to attribute to it autobiographical significance, but I grinned like a clown, making the paint on my face work . . . strange designs begging laughter. Please. Prostitute yourselves in laughter. There. In front of *me*. The poor clown is drunk. Trip. You ask me why I cry and step high in movement too cruel to be merely self-abuse. Working like a shitbeetle in South Africa. 'Boneseed was bad enough, when they introduced that from there it was a crime,' he said, then frowned into the sun along the coast and fingered *Melaleuca*, family Myrtaceae, paper-bark, tea-tree; but truly I *have* forgotten that man. Even when I speak to say hello I have forgotten him and his long legs which strode one step to six of mine, jogging, and his impatience when I decided to dawdle. He wasn't at all like my brother, *except*. A man's a man and there are similarities that hit you right away. And they said to me, 'Well, sister, have *you* ever been raped?' And I said 'Oh no, not me.' It's like I've forgiven all rapists. And the men lean back and relax like roosters when the hens are not, well, asking for it. Hens become a ball of feathers, and wait, you know . . .

So trots conversation.

South Africa has me thinking of Bjelke Petersen and his junket round Tasmania talking about the flag and the Commies coming down and infiltrating and snipping off your balls when you're not looking. I was in Tasmania once and know a thing or two about balls, have seen men pinch each other in cruel sport. And she said to me, patting a puppy on the head, 'Well they're all outside you know, so vulnerable . . . A man can never really be tough, not with that fragile piece of flesh hanging, in a way, defenceless.' 'Oh, yes?' I said. Women have a certain pride when they start thinking about things, well, that could drown you. I see a great big iron jockstrap surrounding Australia like a string of warships and I'm afraid Old Joh is trying hard not to be too defenceless. It's absurd I know but the clown's grinding her teeth outside the window, leering in. They think the machinery's gone bung and employ one hundred men for six months to fix it.

If you asked me why, I'd grin and smile, or grit a smile. Give me a drink. I'll tell you a joke only it's got to be on me, I haven't any talent for the other way around. You said I'd learnt to dance and that was great, last time I refused you thought it was too hard for me. Especially as no one ever knew the topless woman in the David Niven mask and Charlie Chaplin trousers was me at the Bad Taste Party. Diane Arbus wasn't there which is a pity because I'd dearly love to be in a book of freaks, be inside the horror, and glare out from the pages at the discomforture. But Diane joined the ghost train with a suicide ticket... just beyond Luna Park in the rain. 'Bit of a freak herself,' I heard someone say. Of course, she indentified with twins and dwarfs and giants and clowns. Oh yes, Diane must have known what it was to be a clown...

Heavy I know but it's hard to live with a clown in your head. I spend my time trying to find something pretty. Took a camera to the Chemist this morning and bought a film to take some pictures. The roll was gone on garbage cans and bricks and things before I reached the corner. Show a little discipline, kiddo.

No, *all* that *I* want to do is participate in a *democracy* of clowns who *understand my freakouts*, and well, shrug and smile a bit and let things pass. But they don't, of course. Things do terrify us as they pass. The clowns keep the laughter roaring, the pathetic prostitution gnawing into honey-soft flesh of humourlessness, while mortar and shrapnel fall on the fall-out shelter. All courage and cowardice flattened to one desert landscape. Well listening to Bob Dylan from end to end of the string of days can affect the way you write and where you think. I don't think you should ask me why.

2
Eve was keeping her, you understand. Keeping her out of trouble. The story goes something like . . . yes, it was another time in the past tense. The tense or calm past of Ariadne Boston, possibly both. A pedestrian, Ariadne, of the tortoise type which beats the cars and is fleet of foot in the end, having learnt *entirely* what she learnt along the road. That was how she became famous, by being practical not brilliant. If a butterfly she wished to have did cross her path, she caught it. Then wore it, a clearly deserved trophy on her lapel. Preserved moments, indeed, were like solidified rungs on the ladder to her success, her memory and movement one. When Ariadne enters a room, all have a tendency to deride her clothes and manner and even the content of her speech. Ariadne lurches forward regardless, too sensitive to care for compromise.

Ariadne *embarrasses* me. She is another clown. Even Eve has forgotten how she kept her, jester-wife. But Ariadne owns her life, *entirely*.

3
Will I wait for you? Will you come to me, or will I go to you? What will either of us do? Why I know you're as clownishly scared of blushing as I am. When we're together there's laughter. Whatever we do we're covering pains with face paint, making wanting games all over again. Wary of watery grooves and slippery wishing wells. Well kick your shin and wait around, down under the street lamp where I might be passing soon on my way to visit you.

4

Henry and Bob, of course, made an impact on the world that I could not take seriously. Because neither of them, had I happened to share the same block or circle as either at any time, could take me seriously. So for me they were clowns, providing entertainment when my personal plans were far too serious to be really considered worthwhile at all ... laughable, simply laughable. To the world, Henry and Bob aren't clowns at all. No no. (The feet walk through Cliché on quiet days and shout from the mouth, 'The whole fucking civilisation needs a bloody great dose of V.D.' and with friend companion does laugh.) *What's funny?* But the women mothered them, listened, took the butt-end of jokes and loved them. Around the time she slept with Ferlinghetti, she was fond of Miller's energy, honesty and the absoluteness of his cunt envy! Well, of course, said Joan, women have something to live for now, any cause to put your body where your mouth is. It's not worth it, said Bob, won't make no difference. Real clowns aren't haunted by hundreds of hungry eyes; that's a person at the foot of the human race. Walking to toughen my feet, I find the soles are the only part of me feeling matter, all the rest of the skin touches air. She watched him practising for the next gig. I've seen indolent girls sitting on their hands soaking up and sure of their deserts, their cunts being free that evening. Henry says Wow and Bob says Get Out! So choose. There are criminals around and they vote conservative, vote to keep the world corrupt, boys. Oh hell what *can* a man do? I'm going insane. (Henry, you're cute, the way you make love makes *me* feel liberated! Super Social Studies chick Sorbonning it for greater education, but Henry then gives her the slip) ... who would have believed that Ariadne Boston led the world in '67? And not one good thing was said. No one saw Ariadne take refuge in the caves. I came late and viewed her etchings in an intellectual light. That's good, I said, that could lead the world. I backed back through the hollow doorway, needing a bit of bilious coloured sunshine. This clown is drunk and no one laughs. So see me down the road of a Paul Gallico ending, waving *hi lilly hi lilly hi low*, off in search of humour, juggling one blue and two silver balls in clumsy patterns.

5
(The woman was a union organiser's daughter. Her mother had said that her father had no right to have ideals that kept them all hungry. At a political meeting, she hissed to me, 'you know Bjelke Petersen was a conscientious objector when the Japs were bombing Darwin . . . had to work on his Daddy's property.') Don't talk of dead clowns (blood is shed for another reason as well) now the Pied Piper plays the harmonica among ghosts in some West Virginia hills talking blues about the time he burst through doors to post letters. Eagerly. When the heat was bouncing off hot white rocks a clown limped far behind her words and yet was frightened for what was over her shoulder. *The finger of the Black Death.* In the bathroom an image in the mirror says, 'has there ever been a real threat that can't be fixed, or cured?' The walls of personality. And she jerked in a buzz of enthusiasm about, *how was it? closer to you, the you? are you reading yourself into your words?* ending back at A, describing a circle with her forefinger, the track of the ego trip. Bob re-read the Bible backwards with new thoughts behind the ideas. How many people are twisted around on a map in the air? There was the drowning, the snake and the sickness creating tangents to an outside death. And the bullet with no name on it — *those who've seen it say you have to see it to know.* Beneath the Unknown Soldier in a country town's main street interfaced with another clown, a conversation occurred of Bergman intensity. As if the poor statue were a fountain or a well. We shared a mug of thermos tea in silhouette. I probably picked a geranium from the dry council plot, remembering Dylan's kisses . . . stared into her eyes so long nothing was said except *here stand the walls of personality.* But I crossed the street and bought some chips, a lonesome hobo begged two bob with one hand and had four stolen apricots in the other. I *know* you're sentimental, kiddo. What little clown isn't and hates herself for it? Why when the union-lady talked her tale I nearly had tears, and those darting eyes *didn't need* sympathy, a

helpmeet knows where to place her words on the ratatat tele-
tape of effect. She dropped her hands to her lap, sees Ferlinghetti these days only between the covers of a book, says with
wounded pride, 'The truth is I'm lonely. With my face paint
on, the two silver balls in my right hand and the one blue in
my left, I entered the pub for a beer.' She told the *whole* bar
that the secret of life was life itself, no truer lie, etc. Except
there is no equality among the lonely, twisted on a map
described by a forefinger in the air and the absent cobweb of
entanglements . . . But I never stopped them laughing all the
way down the concrete stairs to the basement. Our best friend
had suicided but they looked to me for laughter . . .

Well either you'll come to me or I'll come to you.

6
Here we are again at the end of a circle searching for the join.
But there on the pavement stands Anna Maria Raincoat
startling in red and black perusing the passing parade.
Urgently. See each foot take her weight in quick succession.
Jews following jugglers. Buffalo bleeding Bills. Christ figures
dragged backwards by donkey voters. A covered wagon is
hidden in silks. The creature inside is suspected of giggling in
the middle of cruel games. Which all leaves Anna Maria
nervously strung to the pavement. There was never an edge to
any of her jokes. The table of borders stared at the smarting
end of her enthusiasm, confused. Without even a word of
believable comfort, only *piteous* indictment. The Aboriginal
throws in her lot with the migrants, refugees from
Communism or Fascism bringing freedom in half a dozen
possessions. The Aboriginal knows only the morality of
sharing. Tears come for a moment but Anna Maria Raincoat
finds the soles of her shoes are chewing gum. She continues an
elastic marking time. I stop and hawk the shirt off my back for
two bucks and pass by laughing. The wind disappears and a
mist descends, a violinist playing Vivaldi in F merges beyond
the extremity of his own music. Anna Maria Raincoat whistles

an air, faulty and repetitious, which she feels as whiffs of memory. (Here is the end of all clowns, studying secretly the true Comedie d'el Arte.) Find the clown that is yourself and play only that part in all the plays you do. Oh oh oh, sighs Anna Maria eagerly dreaming through the rain.

Anna Maria and Ariadne stare at one another, lacking sympathy as I proffer coffee across the kitchen table. *Nice* day, I say. And laugh. The clown can weep, yes, but maintain a poker face, no way.

It is my belief since I have become a consciously female writer that we can write nothing superb without some understanding of Woman, a general all-encompassing being, an everywoman, unless we want to write of a sad, isolated, lonely individual who is always described as a victim, hence giving aethestic validity to the world as a male construct.

Five Fingers Exercises

A
Ideas in the mind are birds in the bush — flitting and mating to a music that can't be taped . . . but, draw them in hand? A change comes, roles are reversed, you pick up a pen. You are a trapper, the hunter, a ruthless being who would pluck stuff preserve, become a narrow-minded, thin-lipped collector with buyer's eyes ignoring such beauties as youth and age. 'Why have you called her Celine?' This is Myopic One speaking, his rolled cigarette has gone out and his breathing shows he has been smoking a lot, all the same he is bent with my manila folder on his lap, elbows on chair arms, fingers gently on corners, two knees, beard, hand and hand seem to protect my work and be like a crab — a caring sort of smile. His own mind is as busy as birds in the bush, 'You must read Mr Triple Dot . . .' 'I haven't. She should seem French . . . i don't know it came. Her mother will be a slut punter lady drunk with thick make-up.' 'But read Celine . . .'

'I wish to write a *book*,' i said, 'a book, but i know neither what, nor how.' Months ago Kon suggested, 'Make more pieces about Trudy, Paul and Violet.' A discontinuous narrative did he mean? I may have been thinking when to put the kettle on, whether i would have another cigarette, how this particular social encounter was going, what was underneath it, but definitely i was not thinking *at all*. I do not think, sometimes i am feeble-minded. It was the same day Kon said, 'I don't know whether you are Violet, Paul or Trudy.' I laughed.

Someone came in here the other day and said writers should not have ideas, quoting someone who was agreeing with someone who thought like many others — this constitutes a school of thought — (i certainly would feel more at ease if such were the case, but . . .). Writers by nature are *self-educated*; if retarded by institutions, must set about their self-education later in life, . . . must join the hobos in the reading rooms of public libraries, . . . slink like reviewers of R certificate newspapers, guiltily penniless and undecided, between the shelves of bookshops. My point is so simple it's obvious: can one find what is dearest to one's heart? In other words, can one get away with it? If one does . . . (oh oh oh, i am a romantic — immediately i set the scene, we have come to where i have never come, into the gully where the lyrebirds dance in the month when they dance we are driven and wondering as trees . . . they are not shy of us — we neither hide nor are aggressive . . . maybe we have waited all night and bits of forest have attached themselves to our persons. We have a silence and depth usually associated with still-water ponds — sheer joy. We have passed through the stage of frantic panic, through the senses of guilt and loss, beyond hunger and greed: we stand and wonder.) . . . and if it is such that can be articulated, is this what one writes? One last . . . another question: is it, this knowledge of one's own love, the strength needed or the goal attained?

B

Oh yes i am an angry young woman. (i write that before the bright orange eggs and orange juice of a hungry breakfast . . . among last evening's remains) (But then i ate). There is anger in here inside because i am risible . . . (milk coffee spilt all over the stove and down the gas jets, — oh dear dear.) Trust is apparently a complacency i cannot afford — people are vipers — i don't want them to do anything for me, . . . it's the way they twist their spines to turn around and bite you, . . . to make the cage, then needle you with prongs. You must be suspicious, it is the only way. To think the times to prevent others feeling cages or hurt i've played ignorant, i've let their shoddy little arguments ride roughshod over mine — to make mine as leather as summer feet? (Rancid butter does not fascinate me. The loud lapping and spoon slapping of a sugary milk and cereal plate next door calls up only ugly visions of ferocious greed . . . 'Hands up!' 'I'll give you my money, my life, but but please don't take my sloppy cereal, my fried mashed potatoes or my shower with the bathplug in.' [That sort of hunger.]) I've heard more of Kon; he is asking why i should want to change my style — why should she experiment, why come out of her conventional background? Oh the many and various ways a man can insult you! Why? It is beneath me to answer — perhaps too often it has been beneath me to answer and their ignorance is justified, they have not had the opportunity to see my *anger*. . . of course i've been too cautious. I wanted to learn, not to teach. My desire not to teach must have meant i omitted to teach myself — the subject of myself — to those whom it has been my great good fortune to have met. Oh Kon. You define your own cage and on the wall you have a set of prongs of varying lengths and breadths which you can choose to use on the monkeys passing by, or otherwise you hide, . . . and from your hiding place issues the distant cry 'why?' (Must i get doped on the caffeine content of coffee to have the strength to shout across the acres of white concrete to a possible polar bear in the corner my answer? Do i need a stronger dope? No; do i need to leave you there, pleasantly defined, having gauged the length and breadth of your prongs?) *Why?* (Oh, the sigh of a mountaineer who has the strength and the equipment, but who has not climbed the mountain, yet.) First, the preamble, the get-me-straight-at-the-start-mate: i am not coping, my intentions are far from artificial, i do not want to please you or anyone else; i.e. i am serious and *nothing i do is easy*. The conventional story-prose-narrative style doesn't fit correcty — i get bruised under the arms, have to keep my shoulders in a hunch, thrust my chin forward and down — i have done it, . . . it was difficult and painful, but i could walk out like that, meet the public eye. Meet the people on Lit. Street, but forever in that society i do not want to be misunderstood as a hunchback, not by nature being a hunchback you understand. I have fitted into more hideous contraptions than that to have a look around; a good amateur at disguise, maybe. (I weary, even now — every answer to *why?* from me is 'to find' and every answer to *what?*

is 'being' and *how?* is why i make so many mistakes; another way is: what i have to be is why i do something one way or another.) I am risible, fair enough — but anger is such a desperate animal it has to be tamed or otherwise the irrational rage will sire itself, more desperation and more frustration. The rampage would be quite too frightening. (Now i will clean in the quiet mid-morning of business cars passing.)

C
So pretentious and how long will it take — Joycian twelve years twenty-four hours. Voices. Voices. There are so many voices wishing to speak (— don't ask you who). Voices like persistent lonely people whining banal daydreaming wishful willful nasty-get-your-own-back noises; unfortunately the voice of the prophet — or was it the voice of the gossip, a handy voice whatever — is drowning. Is calling. Is too far away in the sea, its hand like a periscope seen through binoculars (binoculars i am too lazy to adjust to my lopsided eyesight) waving to me, sign-languaging to the blind, wish-complicated looker from the rock; dangling car keys just taken from the lock, locked — safe daydreamer on the rock. What? Don't signal to me Wise Voice i am too lazy i am likely to unlock my car and drive away. Drive towards a landscape i have not seen but which i know intimately through my myths. I am spastically unable to handle and control my voices — these rattles in my ear, trains into tunnels screaming and gone unto destinations (— lazily i throw petals . . . not, so, not, so, not . . . what? The dream. From the embankment i watch, eyes misted against the present, my inspiration rattles away—). In my personal mythical landscape there are officially no trains . . . my myths must lie barely explored. What follows the rattler? Industry (—trappers cattlemen farmers corporation-farmers searchers for oil sellers-of-oil absence of oil — trapped), but i refuse to be industrious. Petals and dandelion chains spelling all magical-siren-like-logic saying, 'make a virtue of your lethargy, your lethargy is you, you are you, not more not less, not, so, not, so, not . . . so; one

o'clock two o'clock . . .) I listen — the voice has no reason; no scheme and discipline: weak notions letting other voices enter, even the voice of the gossip who has not drowned, nor has the prophet yet — the periscopic arm of the voice i should hear waves strangling me with guilt . . . I am a drunken life-saver (— on Bondi Beach, so muscular and brown and ridiculous in his little striped skull cap with tapes over his ears, striding around in see-through speedos *drunk*, rolling drunk, and one of the few thousand who drown every summer is drowning and the people are panicking and the picnickers and sunbathers on the lawn come down and the drunk life-saver just pisses—) What responsibility does the writer have? Voices come on come be me come think me up spend some time sewing me and making me readable. Me read able. Me able to speak, no? Who called? How can I trust you or my eyes — you may be sirens sprites luring me into helltraps — my eyes might make you up (so what?), invent you out of boredom or worse, compensation . . . and when these words are done, what then? Will you i read then smile sigh lie back with satisfaction . . . not, so, not, so . . .

Voices from my invention call me: i have no energy, no skill to save them from whatever fate they fear (— he is terrified of swimming in case it is found that he can . . .) No, this is unacceptable, that the siren-muse should torment *me*: which, who, was it i i i i i i i, sing a thousand voices (—angry meeting of do-gooders all not agreeing on good and what it is to do good — but talk, argue, shout, seethe — they all *care*.) Where can my ear go away from the trains in my ears and the hands in the seas of my landscape: *my* landscape, that inescapable cloud river green grass tree bush area i have all full of words and memories and every damn thing i need (—somewhere unseen?). Away from the sea — it is this, no thirsty desert myth can drink away that sea, in me, but my myth is a landscape and not a wind-sun-summer-sunset washed seascape. *No.*

D

I can't hold writing (. . . my favourite pet has turned into an eel — who plays with the ears of an eel, who sits it on knee garring inarticulate games? — and is slippery and is wriggling and is excited; is otter-busy in an artificial pool). I stand and stare at this agitating movement in my own head (watching an otter-busy eel one can negate all but eyes and empathy, *feel* supple, three-dimensional, agile; but take to speedos and the olympic pool believing oneself to be eel and rude the slow heavy human crawl, the laboured essential breathing!) believing myself able at the typewriter to place it on paper. To merely have the hours and the time. 'Remember to remember,' Kon quoted himself. 'That is one of my lines,' he assured us. Jerked us. Myopic One peered into his knees at close-typed pages there: a wealth of work. Appealing to Kon, appealing to me to know wealth, wealth. 'Magnificent stuff,' thick accent, slapping the words 'ze vords' (—three men met in a park and began walking, 'walking' is repeated in threes a number of times throughout the piece, and as they walked they talked, and in the end they walked abreast — three men, Abel, Babel and Cabel) . . . 'The way you lick the cigarette paper. It's summer again,' says Kon. Meaningfully. It is summer, My. is licking a cigarette paper, but they make it into writing. 'Good line.' 'Not such a good line. But could be a good line. In the right place.' — We are each thinking of our inventions (— this was not talking and walking, this was playing cricket in the park — Kon bowling leg spinners, My. batting and me fielding and throwing it back to Kon — Kon sitting back smiling, commanding and flinging things down and listening) — 'But i find it hard to articulate. Articulation belongs to a social situation and there are so many modifiers, distractors, intervening concerns you do not answer why in conversation . . . perhaps you can clear things up a little?' Nothing is clear, but Kon took my meaning and Myopic One took my meaning; maybe they would wait for me to catch up (—this was an easy game of cricket in the park, for it was an accidental flippancy) (at lunch time i saw builders of a building half built at the university playing cricket like primary school boys with improvised bat and ball — close in sillies, and slips and so on). They are gentle, as i see them now, i should like to write something. My. slaps ze vords and says 'magnificent stuff' and Kon edits and pushes me on . . .

I am tempted to narrate indulgent fictions at this point — fictions in landscapes of my own making, but i have not seen *the world* they come from (my fictions would be at dusk and second hand) England and Europe. They are so different these two . . . In '68 My. was doing his first translations into a language he hardly understood, an expatriate from a land of the German language — a stern combination forcing a man . . . He has a mind possibly mapped in co-ordinate geometry and calculus in which art grows (like a Klee) controlled and at random, symmetrical but far more subtle. A delight to the mind — he knows delights to the mind. He has taken an impossibly idealistic stand against bombshelters and other compromises to man's stupidity and imperfection that man builds into his environment, forcing on future man a legacy of mediocrity, a legacy of compromises (these are of course protection from himself) . . . therefore Myopic One would be a babe in the wood or a revolutionary intellect according to a pattern which seems to reflect chaos but can be seen as symmetry from a view of perfection . . . (— perhaps we are not kind to the German intellectual.) (In a room when the intellects he respects have left, gone away while he is reading his work, Myopic One will look up, look around for the next best contender, adjusting the tiller as it were, pointing his knees to a compass point as near as possible to his desired and continue. He would not stop nor alter the tenor of his words — steam ship.) Kon likes ease, he does not feel threatened by his own indulgence, his work makes a merit of ease and work is his indulgence . . . So. I am different. Perhaps we three will never understand what is easy for the other two.

E

I am desolated: here's the story — (i will not lay the blame so much on me as i deserve — i live don't i, what right have i not to or to live it this way or that, but i do not think i can face these facts). Suddenly it is clear, it is always clearer out of another voice. 'Tell me . . .' he started, and by the way he stopped i saw it was important. Go on! 'Are you still interested in Kon? I mean sexually, because if you are it's no use — he is not interested in you or in your work. He is indifferent to both.' Suddenly it is clear. For a week or two now Kon has run as soon as i come near and i have accused him of all sorts of personality faults and i had become obsessed with his work — his new book, his ideas, his *contribution* — i was looking at them *critically*. I wished to discuss him with anyone who would listen, or speak, but i noticed his blatant avoidance of me. This was complicated, a talk will fix it. If we could have a talk . . . there was jealousy in me too and i enjoyed it as an evil one who sees a snake rear its head before the others and does not mention it . . . if i could get him alone . . . Suddenly it is clear. I am bright, let's forget it. What is he to me, i never laid a claim, never. Never once. But now; haven't i too shuddered when i've seen one with a dreaded emotional attachment approaching, haven't i said through closed lips through the corner of my mouth to the one who is closest 'think of something, get me out of here,' haven't i? and isn't this exactly what Kon has done, every time, every time since . . . He ignored my presence so thoroughly that when i returned to my place i cried for three hours, or was it since . . . I was drunk and i admitted that, that i cried for three hours over him, no i didn't admit it i threw it at him, and walked away; he shrugged, opened his palms, i am innocent; of course you are Kon it's only me, no need to worry. So. Since then or then he has run a mile and i am a fool. Suddenly it is clear. The voice says 'I didn't mean to hurt you, it's a fact.' A fact, of course. Of course.

Now i have risen from the most unsatisfactory coupling ever, in my opinion. On the rebound, this is an old story told a thousand times: you repulse someone, someone repulses you. There is no gift or giving in human intercourse, nor theft. It is beyond our moral control, and yet — here is the crunch, we take full guilt for selfishness, for immorality. We are trapped. I am powerless against Kon's indifference, and yet the only thing i wish to vanquish is the indifference of it. Anything. Anything — i wondered at the stupidity of Lady Caroline Lamb i wondered also with admiration at the power of her passion. My pride wondered. Now i wonder at my pride — so proud i hook my hooked arms around my knees, drop my head and allow no entrance. If you tell your wife, tell her the truth, tell her of my extreme reluctance, tell her of my indifference —

No, not *anything* Kon (if ever you should read this), i am too proud. Struck where all earnest things strike, right at the sense of humour — you construct sparkling brilliant wit crowds of people collapse with laughter the indifferent one is unamused, oh, i have been that indifferent one. Was so before, before i began . . . i began to cry, again, my loneliness and all, there is only one way out, where the truth will come out, here in prose; 'there must be a story here, if not, someone must know somehow.' The passion for indifference, do you remember do you know, is almost as strong as the passion of the loving one for the littlest consideration — as if both did fight a civil war over a lousy patch of desert — Well i will turn away here, i will turn from that part of me which is torn (like tears in the stretched pigskin of a drum). There arrived on my desk a pile of women's poetry books, oh it's good to see, and i come. Goodbye Myopic One, goodbye Kon, goodbye Prince Hamlet . . . Now I write always the capital I.

Why is women's conversation boring? Who says?

Inside us even we say it is. For so much in us is imbued with the male aesthetic. The suspense. The purpose. The point. The revelation. The relentless progress of the plot. Appreciation of this is stamped into our learning programmes and when we read fiction for pleasure we want it. We want to be teased, to be told what happens and then why, how, etc. We want to be made ignorant only to be given intelligence. This is a learned appreciation of a learned aesthetic of a style of story.

The only thing which denies its truth, as indeed it is down there in the emotional response, is our own experience. Looking closely at how we interact — a writer listens, a writer notices — women experience not ignorance then intelligence in their conversations with each other. There is no detection followed by satisfaction — the outflowing breath of satiety, rest. There is, I find, more excitement between women in conversation when the known, the recognised and the apprehended is expressed. This is not followed by a spent sensation at all, rather more a sense of inspiration.

A sense of inspiration yet all was known — perhaps never before articulated, but known certainly.

It is interesting that many women wish to write, perform and film monologues. Djuna Barnes's Nightwood *takes off into an amazing monologue. Stevie Smith. Others. The stream of consciousness has monologuous rhythms. It is not that women wish to tell each other anything. They don't claim to give intelligence. When the aesthetic drive is in gear the women wish to appreciate, to handle with delicacy perhaps a point, an observation, an insight which if given second place to the relentless progress of the plot would be rendered banal, mundane, unimportant. The shimmering jewels of appreciation of what is there would be lost in the flapping veils of what is invented.*

The grand standard of what is acceptable as a story is raised against the knowledge of what she considers beautiful in her own soul — her mind, her aesthetic intentions. There could be turmoil here, a falling between two poles — lack of either aesthetic success.

Even understanding this, it is difficult to achieve it in a literary form. We feel we might be doing the wrong thing — raving on — raving like a hysteric. We have only accuracy, loyalty to perception to rely upon.

And loyalty to daydream, fantasy, moments and emotions so quick in coming and going they might never have been . . .

Except, some other woman nods.

Conversation Without Inverted Commas

Here I am, Nora. And there you are, Clare. Gone plain in our earnestness. Lines gather between our brows — yes we frown. You will have skin cancer. Me? My feet are hard, hard leather. My hairs seemed to grow, then stopped growing. Sometimes silky in the evening sun. Now I wear my trousers rolled to the knee. What, Clare, you no longer have curls about your ears and down your forehead. Your eyes have changed. Oh no, they are still large, but different, they seem more round, more of the eye itself and it is energetic. Remember, Clare, you had sleepy eyes. Languid. Eyes which squashed when you laughed, when your face composed laughter, when you composed gifts of your face. The gifts broke when the Christmas tree fell, in the new year you were giftless — did you say you wasted money on cigarettes, alcohol, coffee and tea, and in the evenings wasted time talking? And yet your talk became impatient, feverish, tormented. You were driven to use the telephone, and at times my phone rang, and the bells were your bells. And I ran. How are you? Not pregnant? Not likely. You don't like the way I use fuck in my conversation, but I don't think you really mind, chiding me was something you could do that was mildly affectionate. Up yours, I say, and ask about him half-heartedly. For him I think there is no hope, for you I am sad, beachcombing won't do, nor having him spoil you, nor . . . Nora you are elusive, you move as swift as a sprite and yet when I meet you or ring you or see you or even think of you, you have not changed. You were too alone to ever stop moving or being the same. What did you preserve yourself for? There was something sacred you only laughed about, I mean you laughed away telling it . . . It was something I couldn't give you, Clare. You were too vulnerable to *him*, and he would have destroyed it. Once I did give you a poem in which I called you Bella, he forced you to burn it. Anyway you could never read poetry, you thought it was some sort of crazy letter: did you? Or was it you who would not tell me where I was going? You did not want to watch, Clare, I don't know, but slowly I go, slowly life pushes me further and further to the edge of the earth — it is both desperate and optimistic. (Behind Nora sees a classroom full of girls in blue uniforms, and their neat handwriting of couped-up hollow words on lined paper — she is sitting on the teacher's desk with a book of Tudors on her knee, she gives the students nothing, she can't even remember the six wives ...) Clare, do you understand? No. Yes, not exactly. My mind can't find — (Clare is by the sea, he is away, she has a new black dog. The beach is deserted and there are cowrie shells by her toes, she is seeing sprites in the waves and slight mists, yet hardly believes the dance she sees with her own eyes. She is bored, even here, where she is happiest. Nora is in front moving away, running or flying — she seems to know). But I am anchorless, adrift. Tides move. Your thread out to me is of thinnest fishing gut, but it slackens and tightens with no rhyme or reason. This puzzles you. Occupies your mind. You go down to the sea, behind the shack you share with him. You have not let you both have children. I know that is your last stand, but I who am adrift would love a child ... Some of us wear gypsy clothes, walk in the city street bare-footed with a baby or a pack on our backs, we swagger. We are outlaws — we must forsake morals and all that which is precious to your *him*. I have many men, Clare, I wish you to know this, I cannot live without them, but one, one, Clare, is too painful. We gypsies do not walk around the streets with men on our backs; and the poverty too, Clare, is another trial, but I could never change it for the spoiling you get from *him*. I would like to hate him but I can't, he is too far away, and it is useless to hate one individual man. Nora, maybe *I* hate him, but if it is that it is easy enough, it is familiar, it gives me rights: my subtle ways of torturing him — I tease him, I make him cry for my own amusement, and then I am disgusted, not with myself but with him. It is a familiar tangle, I've learnt the ropes. (Clare is by the sea, a small fishing port, yachts come, bigger vessels come carrying ore and shellite. Clare knows the ropes and how to sail, she knows her way about the docks and the special terms for tackle. She knows the price of fish in China.) Often I call my hate of him love, and express it, clumsily but well enough for his conviction. You don't know what it's like, Nora! Clare, we wear rags, I can't tell you why, we buy dope instead of clothes, also we like rags . . . how can I explain to you along the strained stretch of this thin thread? and you as equally alive the other end. No matter how far I move to the left edge of the earth, Clare, I am still as feminine as you, I am not becoming a man as I once wished to become — remember I was ambitious? But becoming a woman is as hard anywhere on the earth . . . don't you think? No, Nora, I don't think, when I think I don't know what to think, sometimes I resort to thinking things, I mean stories, tales, gossip, if I think something is unfair, there are also other things unfair and there's such a lot I don't know. *He* is always telling me things, discussing his complaints with me, he respects my mind. It gives me something to do . . . I have not yet thought of suicide, and why should I go? It would destroy him. I'm Nora, I am still searching for those who refuse to be destroyed, is this wrong, Clare? It sounds like an icebox, you are slippery freezing point. No you are colder than I, we are warm, with our rags and our packs and our tough peasants' feet. Why I am crying all the time, do you cry often? He cries I do not, I wouldn't be caught dead . . . I think I understand, it is pride, and a pride you have every right to, you cannot lessen yourself, not in your position. No, I got that clear from the start. (Clare is by the sea playing a line to the clouds.) Give my love to your new black dog, why does our conversation always seem so unreal? I just like to hear your voice, it is always the same, my Nora . . .

Jillian Arbus

It was not as though the name 'Jillian Arbus' was totally strange to her. It was, in fact, the name of one of the most highly respected artists in the country. Janniemedea had seen her work hanging in the gallery, read dry academic articles — 'Jillian Arbus: Artist as Ethician', 'Conservatism and Reform in the Painting of Jillian Arbus', 'Arbus: Birds and Symbols' — and seen her photo in the newspapers now and then supporting minority groups on political issues. She was a public figure, one whose comments were called for on news of cultural interest. Jannie had missed a lecture she'd given at the University but had seen her walking along the path deep in conversation with two men, and decided that her walk was weary and her clothes were rather dull and shapeless. She was frowning. On the strength of these observations, although she had a fascination for the great and famous which she knew to be of abnormal proportions, Janniemedea gave up any notion of making herself known to Jillian Arbus. Her fascination for famous people, especially artists and musicians, caused her hours of morbid daydreaming during which she discovered that she longed to be disillusioned, to find them to be ordinary folk; there would be a passage through the illusion to the real and in the real there would be the seed, the reason for their fame or the quirk of genius.

The dying words of a crazy aunt, a very old piece of paper with vague pencilled words seemed hardly enough reason to interrupt the day of a busy inspired person. Who was she anyway? 'Who am I anyway? Why should I be of interest to a person like that? What will we talk about? I don't know anything about Aunt Sally. Maybe I can ask her how to get to it — the farm I now own. Oh this is ridiculous!' Through the swirls of negative thought Jannie's curiosity was the one thing that was clear. 'I'm curious. About? About the woman.

Strangely I'm not curious about Aunt Sally, she was too much her own statement. Absurd.' So Jannie carried the address around in her pocket, even passed the place several times, searching for the motivating reason. She knew she must go some time or another, and that she would, but she wanted to be there in the right frame of mind, in a state of total receptivity. She, in this case, did not want to rely on her usual effervescence, her controlled and jokey likeability, for the simple reason it set the tone and atmosphere of the conversation; she wanted to be the other, the timid introverted uncertain Janniemedea. She wanted to be accepted and loved by the artist for the defenceless and crude creature beneath, herself. There was a way she was almost certain of being liked, but it was a used method and one which distorted her basic emotional impulses. Among the circle of friends she had fished for and caught she suspected there were some she didn't like very much at all, who in fact bored her silly, who were friends still because of the ongoing dynamics of her popularity. Underneath her quick-witted perceptive chatter, questions were born but not nourished, answers occurred but were discarded in the constant urgency of sociability. She wanted none of this with the artist; trivia was too distracting and confusing; but without it, her ready standby in the world of people, she was afraid. 'I'm afraid. Of being rejected. Of being totally honest, in case I'm judged to be of no consequence.' Anyway there would be no gossip in common. For the three days she had been wandering around with this on her mind, she had not bothered to refresh her perceptions of the artist's work — 'Jillian Arbus', it was the name not the work.

Can you see the almost stencil-like force with which the typewriter places the words on/through the paper? The creative machine churns and threshes like a mass-producer of mulch. The raw material fills the vats and bins, fills bubbly and alive, then settles and becomes dense. Known. The storywriting machine is like an editor neck-deep in the tangled mileage of candid film — films, books, memories, dreams, hopes and fears, love, pain and the whole damn thing, thoughts and sortings-out — haphazard glancings of black and white, technicolour, tints and sepia. Steps over wet pavements with nothing to do but dreaming of meeting someone for emotional excitement, for recognition, for something to do. Passing art galleries and galleries of pretension. Drinking while they play pool in the public bar. Jannie, you see her sitting up. Cracking a joke while her heart's breaking with anxiety to see, to know, to do, to love. Jannie, exactly five foot high, a chubby block of cuddly muscle. Jannie, droll-faced buffoon recounting again adventure this and adventure that; holding inner breath for adventure the future. I see her, her friends have paled to black and white, she wants more. She wants to travel with a knapsack on her back and a mission in her heart, a whistle on her lips and a health she never had. Rain, wind, hail, snow and sleet pasting the fair strands of hair to her glistening apple-cheeked face, and laughter like jewels or dew in the sparkling sun-shower, that humour essential in adversity, that careless bravery of 'who cares about me?'; those with the least to lose protect themselves the most. Those times I was driving up the road bursting with anticipation, noticing everything, alive with the sense of pilgrimage, checking back across the past for the milestones and fingerposts; each decision we make second by second builds the character, creates the temple of identity; the accident, the destiny, the luck mapping each unique and special fate. Here Janniemedea's aunt dies in her arms in the middle of a riot, a torch delivered at the crossroads, a nameless not-even-noble destiny placed in her hands. And her heart burns. She has a burning, passionate, feminine heart, and who wants to know?

Janniemedea had received sexual rebuffs: times when she had laid bare a purely physical need, perhaps gracelessly, perhaps with a hopeless laugh, remained as some of the most desolate on her landscape. They were even more barren than totally unwanted physical embraces in the arms of a stranger after nights of booze and dope, for when the sweaty fog cleared and fell to a seedy grime in her head she felt a resurge of libidinous energy, a sense of herself as both decadent and pure. But wanting and being refused left her nothing but, not even a stinging, humiliation.

Janniemedea dropped into a basement bar where a black woman was scat-singing. She closed her eyes and swung her head to the music.

Janniemedea talked of relationships which ended with breakfast.

Janniemedea visited an old lover who had reached the settling age of thirty, played the old flirtatious word games, and left. Not even depressed.

She visited the garage in which her mother's things were stored, dug deep with the dusty cough, discovered the photographs. And then was quite bored. The river between life and death was too wide.

Janniemedea sat in her flat playing her old country and western records very loud. Humming on her harmonica.

In a junk shop, idling, she stole an ash tray shaped Australia.

About seven one night she knocked on the attic door.

A number of people come to mind as models for the artist. Somehow, perhaps accidentally, perhaps the destination of a deranged wandering in city nights when you're young and romantic, I have Jannie paused in the suspense of the interval between the knock and the answer, where the ears become dog-aware of the giveaway sound, where hints have the importance of revelations, where . . . any fiction writer could give any number of details, and get away with it. Dangerous moments those when you have brought people to the bones of the plot: it's unforgivable to take advantage of a prone reader, unless you're certain of the facts you give. Of course I am uncertain. What happens? Jannie hears some sound inside, so, rather than slow down, her heartbeats speed up. This isn't television, I don't have to tell you the size, shape and texture of the door. A globe above her lights up. She is wearing her anonymous clothes, but even so lets her eyes check and rest on the doormat. She is ignored once the door is opened as a stocky woman younger than Jillian Arbus though older than Janniemedea bursts through the brightly lit entrance, pulling a wool-lined lumber jacket over her shoulders, and, obviously having the last word in an argument, shouts, 'I never said violence was rational. As if anyone could!' Then thunders down the wooden stairs. Big boots. Jannie laughs, and laughing, enters. Feels immediately at home in the spacious, untidy, arty attic.

'What a time to walk in on someone's life! However I can see you're going to stay, it's in the stars. Anybody who arrives in the wake of that windstorm . . . what a troubling person she is. Coffee? Oh this place is such a mess. I haven't enough money to keep a housekeeper. Four times a year it's clean. The seasons. I make it such an unearthly clean place I can't come home for a week. Then I return to an amazing calm, and work. That was a couple of weeks ago. I began a series, and they're wrong, wrong, wrong. I can't do what I set out to do, my arm is too inhibited, too tight, you know? I went to a couple of yoga lessons to loosen up, but my mind was elsewhere. What I need is broken bones . . . I paint things, not shapes. But shapes are very safe you know, open to subjective interpretation. It's a camel, no, it's an elephant. If I painted the actual things they'd recognise them all right, and they'd say obscene, dirty porn. Oh my poor dear you don't know what I'm talking about, do you? It's a breakthrough, but I can't quite break through, if you know what I mean. You're an art student I take it. I used to loathe young female art students, but now you interest me, your arms aren't stiff with age, they're fluid and feminine, all buttocks and bosoms, heh?'

'I'm not an art student, I'm . . .'

'I didn't mean to sound sexist, you understand. Drink her coffee — she didn't touch it, sugar's here.'

'Fabulous sugar basin.'

'Yes, it's a charm. She confuses me, the way her mind works . . . Who, by the way, are you?'

'Jan . . .'

'To say the portrayal of sadness is depressing is . . . a depressing comment. Bad art is depressing, no matter what it portrays. Good art, who can say? She's right though, it is depressing, because it's not good enough. It's out of character, it's out of time with my rhythms, I do not have a fluid Imagist line. And that is just that! Jan, did you say? And you're not an art student? Thank God.'

The pause in the torrent of words was such a shock Janniemedea burst out laughing. Oddly one of the things which contributed to her amusement was one of her mother's famed comments, 'I don't like cats. Whenever you walk into a room they're always jumping off tables'.* Two grey ones were weaving in and out among the condiments on the kitchen table. If they came too close she would begin sneezing. There was a cat-like grace and mischief about Jillian Arbus, too: she was tall and her loose soft-fibred clothes fell in what could be called a sleek way. Her eyes stared but her mobile mouth admitted an unmistakable humour. She seemed to be artlessly acting herself. Cross-legged in a roomy cane chair, she lit a cigarette and waited for Jannie's laughter to abate.

---

*Actually that is one of my friend's stories of his aunt, of whom he says I remind him. But fiction is a thief, Jim, fiction is a thief.

'The truth is I'm Sally Green's niece. You visited her once twenty years ago, and before she died she told me to visit you. It was a while before I could pluck up the . . .'

'That was terrible. I read about it in the papers. She caused a minor riot I believe. Oh you poor dear. I thought it must have been *my* Sarah Emma Green, but I wasn't sure. She swore she'd never come off the property, she had isolated herself from civilisation. She knew the wild. The only people who visited her were crazy, quite crazy. Even though I often think about it, I could never understand. There was an oppressiveness about Sarah, an obsession about the basics of life, a horrid fearlessness. And a purity. The sort of person you want to think about rather than know. I couldn't stand it any longer, I had to come down off that mountain outpost. It took me a long while to settle, and I still find 'getting on' with people difficult. You know I locked that door and it stayed locked for months, and I fought alone with recalcitrant paint and canvas. This whole place was bare boards and blotches of colour, a mattress and an electric kettle. Benzedrine pills. I was manic and as skinny as a stick. My one goal was that first exhibition.'

'I read about it, eighteen years ago you were crucified.'

'Not at all. Instant success. At least what I wanted, recognition, discussion, criticism, argument. I was taken for a serious painter right from that opening. And I was vulnerable, physically and emotionally weak. They could do nothing but strengthen me with their swords and pinpricks. You see I was too raw to know the game of the sycophants, I curled up my hermit's lip at their ignorance and discovered my true friends and colleagues almost at once. Perhaps I was a sacred cow. You know, the type they leave alone all year, then in one big enormous feast they cut her up and eat her.'

Janniemedea was frowning to stop crying. Jillian contemplated her for a moment, then rose, tousled her hair, followed the line of her jaw with her ring-finger, stopped at her chin and let it rest there.

A hum(m)m fills the scene. Jillian Arbus's aura is grey-blue with a war(m)th of pink. At ti(m)es surely violet. (M)ulled wine, ho(m)e-(m)ade bread. (M)ention of sheep-skin chair slings, ca(m)el-coloured carpet. Aro(m)atic s(m)oke fro(m) gu(m)-scented leaves (m)isting through the bush, (m)oo-cows grazing. A(m)ong the (m)ounds where (m)other found (m)e snoozing and I rode ho(m)e in her ar(m)s with (m)y nose on her boso(m). In (m)y nose re(m)ains the s(m)ell of wo(m)an. Hold (m)e. M(m)me.

Jannie's head reached Jillian's shoulder and it hung lower as she hugged.

Each day the women came to drink at that well, and each day they were new women. The women were unknown to each other every day. Perhaps it is an abstract 'place'. However the first mentions a lovely word, listen. The sibilant sound is taken up in small water-like surges among the group which becomes a well swishing *listen*. The well is a whirlpool and a spiral energy turns them round and round, searching the others' faces, seeing the rheumy eyes of age, the sharp startled stars of youth, the lurking fire in the dark calm of middle womanhood. The eyes become the birds which sing. And indeed the birds have much to sing about for the forest is full of fruit and berries drip their juices on to the leaves which then are sticky. A bride is seen escaping in terror. The effect of the frail white lace of the veil, smaller and more torn in each successive painting, is to pull the viewers' eyes closer and closer to the frame, an enigmatic and disturbing ruse causing frowns.

As if in answer to the frowns the bride comes on a desert scene, her veil is black coarse cloth. And a raven in the picture is also black. Soon it is evident she is a nun with child, hugely surveying the sand, the wind has caught her headdress and it is majestic. The storm grows, the violent veil obliterates her face but half an eye, the piety has gone from that small slit. The ravens have multiplied. There is not such a harsh contrast between the deserts ochre and the sky's blue. Unnoticed the ravens on the sandhills become a camel train and the woman recedes deeper into the softening colour. The camels carry riches and the men are happy for they are nearing the end of their journey. And at the oasis they visit prostitutes and drink from kid wine-skins. The woman has her child with her now.

There followed a series of horrifying portraits. ('I had a terrible tooth at the time, and fell for commissions.')

What can you say? Janniemedea stared at the slide-projector after the light was switched on, reached blindly for a cigarette. Jillian was vulnerable, she knew. She fiddled with a light bulb and boxes and boxes of slides, and was jumpily attentive to every sound Jannie made, she cleared her throat and started, 'Why . . . I saw. I painted what I saw, and I saw those sorts of things in their eyes, in their posture, in their clothes. Perversions, cynicism, lust, sadism. They blamed it on me of course. But in a handsome face I would see a particularly cruel line tracing its way around the mouth somewhere. That line would fascinate me, the more disguised it was by good humour and learnt graces the more it would fascinate me, the more I was challenged to find connecting links between the inside and the outside. I had to throw a lot of the suggestions of the line into the background, find images. Birds, in feathers of finery pecking out the eyes of a lamb, for instance. It was around the giveaway line that I built my portraits, it took on a diabolical beauty, and I would argue that my portrait were beautiful, were bringing out the beauty in men — I didn't bother to portray women — and, of course, a lot of people agreed with me, after all I knew a lot more than they did. But my critics saw depths of witchery in my vision: how could such stately visages be seen by anybody who was not a witch, as such demons? And all the time I was only painting what I saw.'

Janniemedea was speechless and the only words she could pick out of the rich swirl of impressions bubbling like thick porridge in her mind were 'I'm too dumb, too dumb'; not that she entirely believed them, but they were the words. Jillian looked at her, smiled and said, 'Have you ever cooked?' Without waiting for an answer she continues, 'my Pagliacci, my crying clown is the hungry cook. As I am an artist of the sight she is an artist of the taste but marvellously and tragically it is everyday and taken for granted. I've been too busy to be that cook, but I've done enough to have a hint. When you prepare meals you imagine the taste, you're so sensitive and careful as you inspect textures and heat, as you inspect your memory for a finished taste-understanding of each and every ingredient, too much salt destroys, too little creates a negative blandness like a wet blanket, and so on. Now really look at the difference between eating a meal prepared by yourself and a meal prepared by someone else, the magic goes — a cold sword of objective criticism comes to play in your taste. Do you know what I mean?' Jannie nodded. 'The meals being the same or equivalent in their majesty, in the one instance you would kiss the feet of the excellent chef, in the next you look eagerly into the eyes of your dinner guests and settle for polite sociability or the excuse that they have a stomach ulcer or had fish and chips on the way over not thinking that it was a dinner invitation. See? So too with painting. All your life.'

'Did you have the child?' asked Jannie, seemingly unaware of the irrelevance of the question. Jillian took the plug of the projector out of the socket, sighed before she answered. 'I've had three abortions . . .'

'I didn't mean to sound sentimental . . .'

'No.'

An ornamental grapevine supported by a trestle fence and several three-inch beams overhead enclosed a small concrete balcony which was vivid with potted plants beyond the bedroom section of Jillian Arbus's large attic space. The smaller grey cat played with the plants, elegantly, lifting himself up on two legs, hardly disturbing the leaves; the other, neatly balanced on the back of the old couch, took note, then returned to cleaning her back legs. But the attention of both Jillian and Janniemedea was centred on Meg Strahan, who sat on the end of the bed thrusting the fingers of her left hand through her short curly hair. 'It's like a Saturday night screw, isn't it?'

When I feel confident to continue and have Meg Strahan introduce Janniemedea to sexual politics, in a personal and pungent way, Meg, the newborn, a name in an unfinished fiction, will refuse. Point-blank. She is beyond explaining where she is, she is impatient with that now worn detail. She wants new action, and hence says sentences brilliant and riddle-like. That it had been raining was evident in her hair; her six-year-old child was tired and grumpy from the frenetic and cold walk which had brought them to the artist's studio when Jannie was sipping tea discussing painting with the painter. Jillian, as usual, fussed, thought of food and a warming drink. The dog lay his bulk by the door. The child, simply, was rude until she asked for textas and drawing paper.

I leave this chapter with loose ends, like unbrushed hair, like my desk which is a mess, like my mind confused butting like a nanny goat on a rope . . . at the beginning Jillian was troubled about a breakthrough she was on the verge of, and Jannie was there to see the fine woman peaking at the blossom of her early forties. I leave her now, staring hard at the troubled drawing of the child. She sees a tight tiny crucifixion stuck on a black ball enclosed by a free shape which is an egg. Flowers and music and smoke-belching chimneys emerge from delightfully free scribble lines. I leave Jillian staring at this by her feet on the floor, in her two hands coffee mugs, and in the background an intense murmuring between Meg and Janniemedea, and further behind the two cats eye the dog.

Seven Abortions

An Indian I think. The dark visitor to your den. Your soul is dark. You spoke to me of souls and loves and I was a juggler of axioms, premises, clichés, proposition x in ratio to proposition y in my mind. My skillful clown kept me there, kept me mellow. And then I played table tennis with your voice. You must be forty. But your meek and mild, adolescent, cheap catholic boarding school, goodie-goodie, clean-the-blackboard voice belies it. Your age. (Hindsight: she is in fact — god help us and county cork — only five years older than myself.) You whined was I in. There I was kissing my Nasturtiums. You asked me about my window box, but you had come to find some confessions in the corner. Phrenologically I had my suspicions — the thin down-turning mouth — aha.

'Your friend is he married?'

'Yes.'

The nose drew in air with such force that your nostrils became one hole; as for the rest it was lipless. (Oh yes my friend he is married, and he is in love with the proposition that he and I be friends. He listens to blues and writes to me, he sends me flowers, and I practise love letters in purple and pink and send them to him. He and I are in love with charades.) But I can see you live dangerously. With germs. It is difficult for me to distinguish between your dresses and your dressing gown. The time of day is no help; no help at all.

'You must be careful. Love is a sacred thing. Love sanctified by marriage . . .'

'(and what could I do?) Ha ha ha.'

'Nothing is sacred any more . . .'

(Reader, I am sorry I am quite unable to relate this monologue, but you can find it in *The Plague*, if you have to, if you can bear it.)

You are making my room into a perilous place. (Allegory: an old old woman in a dim city chapel fell in love with a clay christ, the work of an inspired and skillful sculptor. Each day she sat in the dusty shafts of Gothic light, among the quiet continual movement, the emptying, the filling, the flowered hats. The clay christ's gaze was unswerving and warmed her . . .)

'Every morning her eyes are puffy . . .'

'Whose?'

'Haven't you met Felicity yet?'

'Felicity. Oh yes? (Big ears.)'

'When her sister was in that room with her! The two of them! Shocking! Going all night. Different men. And have you seen the types?'

'Bank tellers. Fashion conscious.'

(I did have to say something and mercy be I am observant.)

'All they ever think about is their clitoris.'

(Well!)

You went on. You didn't even blush at your own use of words. You loved it. And clinical terms stood up like obscene doodles in the margin. You used them more and more often. The more I blushed.

'She was dried up. She was worn out. She was rich. Oh she looked smart. She us(hiss)ed men.'

'Who?'

'Oh an actress I flatted with in Sydney. One day she came to me and told me she was upset. She was pregnant. We talked and she told me she had had seven abortions in one womb! I left the flat the next day.'

'Why?'

'She was too selfish to have children.'

'No. Why did you leave the flat?'

'She was a murderer! Seven beings were denied the sight of God.'

'But . . .'

'I was hurt.'

'But . . .'

'It gives God pain.'

Your body is huge. You have arms that are — I calculate — twenty-two and a half inches in circumference. They flap. As if the hairs in the pits are clammy. There is a sense of evil in my room. What with the Nasturtiums. I feel awful. 'Get out!' I didn't tell you to get out. The evil I feel is finer and more insidious than backyard abortions. Your soul is black. The clown in my mind has dropped his balls. I am defenceless. (I am not defenceless. There is an opalescent pool. Aqua shallows. Sunny beach. Miraculously deserted. It was a beach I once loved on. Too few have done that. Beneath cumulus. Memory and the moment, three hours before it was urgent.

Eyes. Her eyes, we gazed. The actress and I in the pub. Her look was opalescent and quite expressionless.) The Indian comes at odd hours. He is a Sikh. And you and he eat curries. Hot curries in your den. (Foresight: on the day of my arrival, with a curiosity peculiar to that time, the brown scapula of Mt Carmel lazing in the deep white cleft beneath the grubby chenille and on hearing her pathetic typing, I deduced she was fond of G.K. Chesterton, Aquinas, probably Paul, was writing her memoirs and drawing a social security cheque.) In the talk that is going on meanwhile you have revealed that you know a lot about God. You have picked the eyes out of comparative religions. (Allegory: it is the clay that matters. The clay itself is love — the meeting point of Christ, sculptor and old old woman.)

Your small eyes, your little pins, your Brontosaurus mosquitoes, buzz up and down my torso. My nice arms and legs and face don't get a look in. My nipples — glory be to God — stay soft. (Insight: she has checked my washing on the line. No bra. Ha.) I want to lie to you. I will lie to you. I am holier than thou to you. My catholic boarding school was more expensive than yours, and I know all about faith, hope and charity in Greek. And the crusades. And the Schism. And the theological angle on the Old Testament. I know a lot. I'm going to bulldoze you from both sides. Merlin and Nostradamus in one fell clap. You declaim. You shout.

'The Lord will vomit forth the luke warm. Be thou hot or cold.'

(I know not what I do. In my time I have loved many men and many women, many real and many fictional, many living people and many dead, many faces in the crowd. I love the clay. I love the actress and the character she plays. I love her. She is sculpted clay. She shows me the sufferings of the most evil of women so that I am in tears.) You are pleased when you see me blush. The Indian he's too black to blush. You're so pleased. You flatulate fumes into my room. And then you talk of the smell of the garlic in a crowded bus in Castille and how they never open the windows. And how you're sick. And how you've been more down and out in Paris and London than George Orwell. And how you have to get oxygen in the middle of the night, and that's how you count the fuckings. You sniff behind the curtains in my room. You're so heavy I can't move you out of my room. And besides I am dumb.

'Repent.'

You have a bunch of confessions in your podgy mit. (Allegory: one day a fat lady strode into the dim city chapel and knocked over the clay christ with her bulk. The old woman never returned.) You wheeze down the stairs. (The actress has the grand manner and beautiful voice of her class, the odd smile, the expressionless look, the lonely humility. She smokes in a taxi at 3 a.m.)

'You killed my clown.'

And because you killed my seven dwarfs and my Nasturtiums, I re-address the cheques from the Treasury to the Spanish Embassy with glee.

Circles, we imagine as spirals, because the difference and familiarity grow separate or cling together, vary to a relativity that is not mathematical. The element of total surprise seems to decrease. That end, the mere finality, eludes, becomes implosion more inexplicable than explosion. There is a constant movement from which we find no rest, only repeated bouts of restlessness.

Bloomsbury's Son

Violet and Trudy meet after many years: time, how do we view it? Violet has grown to love the beautiful things, but nothing has changed in Trudy's eyes, they are as absorbent as ever. The spectacles make them sharper, she has even been (in a certain angle of light) mistaken for shrewd! I do not mention the times anger has struck and her eyes have flashed. This is natural electricity: to be expected yet a surprise, a shock. She is not so plump, Violet notices, even though they may well have been the same jeans (clean tight jeans, she is a cushion, springier than before).

Violet is unsettled by this grey-haired teenager from the past. Nodding yes *yes*, affirmation of the tiny things she sees second by second. They talk philosophy as a matter of course — the *eternal yea* — we view the time that has passed as either a lessening or an increasing of our doubts. Violet passionately loves beautiful things. They are so. She is elite. Trudy lives in a loft, has taken care never to judge, has taken care not to deal life into two piles, the beautiful and the ugly (the beast has come to her loft to make love — she has doubts about many things).

An overwhelming question rolls over Trudy and Violet, their shoulders tense and it passes — the one look, *the* accompanying look passes from the brown eyes to the blue and before it comes to either a positive or a negative conclusion it is passed back to the brown. There it — the unanswered double-asked question — swims. In eyes like a chocolate ocean. That is Violet, whether such questions endure or drown there is never known. They move into another room.

A roaming plays at the bottom of Violet's beautiful skirt, discreet as the charm of the bourgeois, causing a memory of French films (French is in fact one of Violet's seven languages which judging by her English would be pedantically correct in grammar and atrocious in accent) — there is Danish stainless steel, sterling silver, a huge ring among large rings on her fingers and about her wrists and neck. She plays with these, and yet about her is a clumsiness, a sloppiness even — a carelessness that is not intended indicating that perhaps beyond the evident good taste, there is a basic vulgarity. An earthiness of which Trudy would be incapable. Trudy is ready with tears and sympathy, ready to panic, ready to be as close to tragedy as one can get who will always remain safe. Violet ignores sympathy. Violet loves only beautiful things. But it is Violet who could be at any moment thrust through the brittle crystal shield of her self-protection into the title role of tragedy.

Trudy is aware of breakability.

Violet shines in black crepe and silver. Trudy is a cotton girl.

'You have been brilliantly successful Violet, but it doesn't surprise me.'

This is said badly by Trudy who is actually more surprised than Violet herself. But everything surprises Trudy, life surprises Trudy. Life is The Great Unexpected. She chose 'surprised' from any number of words which might convey what she was saying or something different. Like clay, words are mud pies or pottery. In confusion and on a deeper plane because she wants to analyse what she has picked up, Trudy looks at her fingernails. Violet is silent.

'What's happened to Paul? Do you hear from Paul?'

'Apparently he's become a slut.'

'What!'

'In a bed-sitter just west of London . . .'

'How do you know? Does he write?'

'No, Jonathon Koch visited him . . . apparently he haunts public toilets, competing with David Flowers, how many a night, that sort of thing . . .'

'Oh no!'

('You really have no idea my dear . . . in a dreary alley off Drury Lane . . . Mon Dieu! So depressing and I had just been on the stinking underground . . . pugh! English people just do not wash enough, it's a proven fact . . . In the dreariest room of the most depressing building. My dear! I knocked on the door, and a huge shadow came prowling up behind the glass . . . well I know I'm small, but this enormous negro opened the door and peered down at me, I asked about Paul and he said "no he's not here but why don't you come in?"' Violet and her husband laughed. 'I disappeared as fast as I could and this yowling followed me down the stairs. I had cold shivers all running up and down my back. Oh dear!')

Paul, Trudy tries to really remember Paul, to imagine Paul. Neither she nor Violet have travelled to London yet, for them it is blank and dead and foreign.

What is the past then? But Trudy shakes this question away knowing Violet will think it ridiculous, she shrugs, raises her eyebrows, worries. Will see Paul when she is in London. Violet promptly forgets him, he is dismissed.

Violet has a passion for beautiful things.

Moreton Bay Fig

Thirty years of life on this earth separated the two women who paused together beneath the Moreton Bay fig tree to watch a grey-feathered magpie scratch the roots and rustle in the fallen leaves; and from the older to the younger passed the information that this was a young bird. The two walked across the park, and the trees which might have been ignored by the younger before became magnified in their gross complexity of gnarled veins and sinews — one can assume the younger will not forget the size and shape of a Moreton Bay Fig.

It was a grand occasion. Worthy of the Romantics of Balliol or Magdalen, worthy, I mean, of the honour of time, worthy of a note in one or other biography and a footnote saying, 'March, 1972, Adelaide', was this moment, this short ten-minute stroll, whereby the sun of Inspiration was harnessed by a brief mirror to burn indelible companionship on to the souls of the two simple women. Simple? Simply, two women, an older and a younger one.

The ins and outs of love flirted with her thought patterns, thought patterns which may indeed have been emotions, so highly charged were they with passion — reality-battered incredulousness — possibility swallowed the impossible — the person was met! The studied-one, the one referred to in tutorials by her surname — which was common, it was Smith — the one who had contributed so much to the descriptive Romance of Australia, the one who got her nose so close to the dirt of the land that she could literally smell the past, bring alive the past, hear its rhythms and work at her desk quietly on its rhymes, one of such impact on Australians that people were impelled to ask: why is she called Hilda Smith? what does she eat for breakfast? who are her lovers? what are her mysteries? Now that her work was set among the cultural monuments in the public place, she deserved no privacy; while she was still living they had to file through the masonry of her poetic achievement to attack the living meat in the centre. The younger, too, had come to suck the blood of fame, to feed her monster of ambition and sentiment that consumed, when it was hungry, the emotions and the thought patterns and the sexual tensions of an otherwise healthy, energetic woman, surrounding its greed with the semi-lurid gloss of illusion, the sirensound of promise, the satisfaction of a self-engrossed world. The preoccupation with one's own Specialness was something one could take wherever one went. The glorified monster had brought her here to the simple reality of being ankle deep in crisp brown leaves with a little woman called Hilda Smith (who were her lovers? what did she have for breakfast? and why 'Smith'?).

She slowly unbuttoned her shirt and showed the monster, and Hilda replied, Yes, I know you are a vampire. In other words, I know you are ridiculous and ordinary, but you're wearing your heart on your sleeve and I like it. It's brimming with blood that will eventually fall on the pavements and attract the attention of passers-by. You are what you want to be and you shall be onlooked-upon. I understand. I am, of course, the prophet they think I am. My lovers, well, I spent a night in a motel on the way here with a young boy — the poet lad who does my garden in a ramshackle sort of way — and we made love. It is irrelevant that we love, but our making love, that's relevant, isn't it? For breakfast, well, I must have the radio and the newspaper. I have bran for roughage, tea and toast, a piece of fruit or fruit juice, and a cigarette rolled from my own packet of Drum, which I do not keep in a silver box or a leather pouch or a rubber ring automatique, but how it came, and goes with bits of tobacco stuck to the sticky tape. Another thing, onions scream when they're pulled from the ground . . . of course. What is important about me for you, or you for me, my dear, is merely that we have met. And you in the next few months will write poems about how I am your spiritual mother, how I play Ulysses to your Telemachus, you will be classical and ill-informed — just as you recognised neither the fledgling magpie nor the great old man of Australian flora, the Moreton Bay Fig — but you will be seeking indulgence, which because I know your weaknesses so well I will give, and I will accept your fumbling, clumsy flattery, you will be a guest in my home and I will tolerate your nervousness with sufficient impatience for you to regain your confidence. For confident you are, my dear, underneath your crippling greed. It is the confidence of the middle class.

> When the words had all been spoken,
>   in the rustling of the leaves and the warble on
>   the wind,
> in the whispers from the future and the singings
>   from the past,
> in the long forgotten memory of a biographer
>   yet unborn,
> but keen as mustard surely among the papers
>   left posthumously,
> the rustling of these papers is the rustle of these
>   leaves;
> those whose interest lives can read and love in
>   private
> these ladies dead and gone. But now they shook
> hands, said goodbye at the gate, and that was that.

The younger one paced back across the park. It was sunset. The trees she strode beneath were large significant creatures in the stage set of her fairytale. How does one applaud a significant moment? I have reached a romantic peak, I am as Sir Edmund Hilary at the top isolated on chilly heights. That I am lonely is evidence that I am there. It is a price I will have to pay.

Twenty-four Hours From Tulsa

I drew in at a roadhouse, asked for petrol and went in to eat. I quite like eating alone at a public eating place.

Three tables were occupied by groups of people eating. Three men in white collars quietly and seriously were attacking huge plates of steaks and eggs. Occasionally they offered each other comments about business. Three loud and cheerful truckies lolled at the table to the left of the white collars. They passed good natured congratulations to the waitress, whom they knew and who apparently had just got engaged. She, an ordinary girl with pretty eyes and slim legs, was spending too much time with them. Irrationally I was stabbed by pangs of impatience. I wasn't really hungry.

Behind me two women sat.

I ordered and got up, went to the toilet.

When I returned, my table had been taken by a pair of couples, who had already settled down — cigarettes and matches and handbags on the table, coats on the backs of chairs. I was obliged to take the small table beside that of the two women.

They caught my attention and interest. I smiled at my luck for I had been bored. For the last two hundred miles I had been bored, and the last two hundred nights.

The taller one had a long face, her semi-sneering eyes set wide apart. Her mouth was caught up at the corners. Her hair was long and black, an irregular fringe straggled across her forehead. She wore black jeans and her light tan shirt was tucked into the hipster waist. A short suede jacket hung neatly on the back of her chair. She sat cross-legged at the table, her chin resting on the hand which held her cigarette. Her eyes wandered slowly about the room, always coming back to focus on her companion.

The face of her companion was remarkable for its whiteness. The eyes were blue and frightened. Her mouth was big, and she had large white teeth. The dark hair was straight and short, the fringe cut straight along the line of her eyebrows. She wore a blue twin-set, a pendant of small stones hung on her left breast because she was leaning that way most of the time. She smoked nervously and quickly, sucking heavily on each drag. She did most of the talking.

They must have arrived just before me because our food was delivered about the same time. I enjoyed my soup and sandwiches more than I had thought I would. I had stopped out of a sense of duty to eat, and it was eight o'clock in the evening.

The smaller one stopped her agitated talk to hoe full-heartedly into her plate of hamburgers and chips. The other sipped black coffee and nibbled at raw tomato, cheese and biscuits. Her slow eyes followed the progress of the waitress around the tables, to the counter, back to some table and then banging heavy-laden through the swinging doors to the kitchen.

I got up clumsily. I felt her eyes follow me as I went to the counter to buy packets of cigarettes and matches, and a chocolate to eat with my unsweetened coffee. As I sat I looked her full in the face over the bent eating head of her companion. Her eyes said nothing more but continued unwavering their silent message.

I relaxed, tracing the loose ends of my dreams, which formed and unformed, crashed and recreated themselves, during my lone two hundred mile drive to the roadhouse. The plans I had formed of this journey seemed suddenly impractical. It wasn't that I was no longer game, I told myself, it was just that I wasn't interested anymore. The past is the past, but is it past? As a historian I could not believe in the crucifixion of the past. Its death.

They paid their bill and got up. She swung her jacket over her shoulder, moved the other chair at my table, looked languidly for my eyes and the creases at the corners of her mouth deepened. The other busily purchased a box of minties. They consulted together at the door and turned back to me across a now empty restaurant room. The smaller one smiled broadly.

I sat a while to gather myself. I was a mess, a lonely mess of ancient ruins jutting out where no one would build anyway. If one looked closely, there in the sandstone, one would uncover a beauty. For my life had been the haphazard collecting of beauty: the beauties of the past stacked together to make an ever unfinished temple of learning. That was the way it was with me, with my unwanted history. My study of history was bugged by the present, my present. My person would never admit a present, it was always past or future. Thus I travelled. I travelled away from halls of documents; I travelled away from my beating emotion when I sat down to read. I did the past no justice because I veiled it with my inevitable half-woven shroud of the future.

It was quarter to nine by my watch. I had decided to keep going, the later and more desperate my arrival the better.

The light inside my car was on. The garage man shrugged his shoulders as I paid him. The new attack of boredom I suffered abated and I prepared myself to be bothered.

I lit a cigarette in front of the bonnet and saw that the taller woman was in the middle of the front seat and white face white teeth had her elbow out the passenger's window. She smiled but they were involved in a conversation of their own.

I got in, turned the ignition and started on the way I was going.

'We're hitchhiking. Knew you wouldn't mind.'

'How did you know which way I was going?' I regretted asking this as soon as I did. I could have been more dramatic, at least, more interesting.

'Oh, we don't mind.' It was the smaller and she giggled. She was about to begin on a long explanation of everything, but the one beside me silenced her with a look or a frown; I didn't see.

'There are guitars on my back seat. Are you singers?'

'Composers.'

'We sing, too,' and she giggled again.

I was beginning to be annoyed by black-jeans's silence.

'Maybe I've heard of you. What are your names?'

'You will . . . Why don't you stop at this pub and I'll shout you to a drink?'

'Okay.' I turned and smiled, hoping for a change of expression on her face. Her eyes widened, she raised one eyebrow and the crease my side of her mouth deepened to a crack.

It was one of those pubs in New South Wales that are just on the side of the highway, apparently unaccompanied by any population. It was difficult to see the roof in the dark but I thought it must have been dark brown and steep because the white brickwork was edged at the windows by tasteful chocolate brown woodwork. The main bar in the modern tudor style had a lacquered brick floor, a huge fireplace and whitewashed walls; the top-shelf bottles were backed by a mirror. We went through to the lounge which had large woollen rugs on the brickwork floor and comfortable chairs.

I always feel happier in an atmosphere of taste, and I could see that my black-jeaned friend felt the same. Blue twin-set had hurried off to the ladies.

'My name's Zoe Griffith . . . Her name's Sally Woodcliffe. And what'll you drink?'

'Whisky and water, please.'

My tongue was getting sore from too much smoking. I felt like a drink. Many drinks. The sequence of daydreams and thoughts had crashed again. Suddenly I didn't know what to do with my hands. Thin long slim ugliness flattered me a second. I relaxed. I'm boss. I'm running away. I'm running towards. I'm here, for God's sake. Stay still, still in the present a while. It is ironic, I thought, what I'm running away from and towards is here, here in the present, though with different hair, face and clothes.

I met the smile face on, as she returned with the drinks. Her legs were narrow, she walked with grace. She walked with confidence. I must have given myself away somehow: my walk, my clothes, my eyes?

'Who was she?' she asked slightly embarrassed.

'Who?'

'I know my kind of woman. Our kind, yours and mine, we walk into pubs alone, drink whisky, eat alone in roadhouses, enjoy to observe, ever dreaming, interpreting. Going some place always, thinking too much. Too much. Because what we think isn't too healthy for us. I saw your thought in your eyes just now.'

She tousled my hair.

'Where are you going, my sad ponderer?'

I was confused for I was going back. I had been away trying to forget them, the fringe dwellers of society. I knew I could never forget, but I had thought that with my history and religion I could overcome the twist in my make-up. But away also I had fallen, the fault this time not being education, but my own emotional need, want then desperate desire. I was going back to where I belonged, to the Australian ghettos where loneliness is drowned and laughed at, and principles, if at all existent, are free.

'Don't you see,' I cried. 'I like things right and proper. Healthy. I like beauty and ordered things. A society non-decadent, a happy society, not a society searching for drugs and thrills to keep at bay the boredom of living.'

The other had returned. They touched hands. Sally, quieter, set about drinking her brandy, lime and soda.

'Do you think anybody today has this utopian life you dream of?'

Her eyes narrowed and looked sceptical as she held her cigarette close to her mouth.

'Many people have their happiness. And I think every woman has a right during her life, a chance during her life, to have happiness. But when you don't fit neatly into the square hole of normality, you carry the burden of all the sins of a whole society.'

'What is your work?' she said as though she was no longer interested in society, and as she lit her friend's cigarette. The frightened-eyed friend winked at me.

'History,' I said, and felt hopeless.

'Then you should know that society has an innate inability to be perfect. And what about the individual, can she be perfect, do you think?'

She was looking at the wall. She had pronounced 'perfect' with sarcasm. Sally was looking at her with admiration, and I knew because of that look that they were not lovers.

'Zoe writes poetry,' Sally said with amusement. 'We sing it sometimes. But most of all she has a soft deep voice. We go well together.'

'The past isn't perfect, though some ages, with the rotten things forgotten . . .' I was talking slowly as if to myself. Then with energy, 'The present is never perfect. Only in the future there is perfection. That, by the way, is where I am going.'

She smiled and touched my arm.

'That's where you are wrong. The present is the only time that can be perfect. Have you never had perfection of the instant?'

It was then I drank her in with my gaze. My heart bumped and bounced. Her lips pursed as the corners of her mouth creased.

Sally blue twin-set had been over at the bar buying more drinks. I met her casual glance at us. I noticed her limp now and her age, which must have been about thirty. Zoe was a good deal younger. Perhaps younger than me.

'I've been thinking, Zoe,' Sally started. 'I will go back to Tony. He's not much of a husband, but I'd rather like him tonight.'

Zoe kept smoking and looking straight ahead. I felt awkward. I thought of all their gear on the back seat of my car, and where we were and the time, eleven o'clock, the day and the date.

Then with sudden energy, Zoe said, 'Okay. What'll you do, stay here the night and hitch back to Canberra tomorrow morning? Here's some money. You should never have come, you aren't happy on the road. You keep singing with that group of yours, keep going home too late to a drunken husband.'

She went and got Sally's things from the car, checked her in, and came and faced me.

'Well, are we going? Going back to the future?'

In the shadows outside the pub we kissed. As our legs interlocked and pressed, all the pleasures I had known in the past rushed back and promised more.

I turned the car back the way we had come.

One day I said to myself, I have been carrying these poems around with me for fifteen years now and they are still the same. In the same folder. With the same glaring lack of complete achievement. Within each of the 500 or so poems there was a spark. And for that spark, those 500 little match-flare sparks, I had carried, year after year, heavy cartons of old dirty paper, for most of the poems were typed out on different typewriters and some were still attached to rejection slips with printed logos and compliments. Many had been collected into imaginary slim volumes with special folders and possible names crossed out. Likely titles changed with the colour of the years, the fashions of the times. But the poems, many rewritten yet still retaining the spark, the match-flare, were the same. The fifteen years were 1965 to 1980; my output seemed enormous.

I contemplated this waste — the waste of energy needed in dragging them around — the desperately needed space they took up, not only in my little rented rooms, but in that part of my head which deals with my responsibility to myself and my creativity, and said something like, well I'm not going to take it anymore. Dammit.

So I burnt them. I read each one as I consigned it to the flames and said goodbye as if to pets. I won't say it was a sad day.

Many women who have loved their work and suffered much hassle and privations to do it, have had no choice in the matter of the loss, disappearance or destruction of their work.

Goodbye Prince Hamlet:
The New Australian Women's Poetry

> *Ham: Lady, shall I lie in your lap?*
> *Oph: No, my lord.*
> *Ham: I mean, my head upon your lap?*
> *Oph: Aye, my lord.*
> *Ham: That's a fair thought to lie between maids' legs.*
> *Oph: What is, my lord?*
> *Ham: Nothing.*
>
> (Act III, sc. ii)

Mary Wollstonecraft was making her stand as Australia began: so was Spinning Jenny — from the cottage to the factory, worker in the mill, worker in the house — in short, the modern world had begun to grind, with its troubles and its revolutions. I might even suggest Australia grew out of this major mutation of Western society, or could not have grown without it . . . But see the woman, hear her sigh and above the sigh the possums on the roof. What is she doing? She carries a lamp, her pace has changed, plainly she is too exhausted after the day to bustle anymore — she comes to the kitchen, places the lamp, sits, elbows to the haired wood of her own scrubbing, but why is she not in bed? What does she open with careful hands and shift into the circle of light? Why does she smile, frown, in quick succession? As she reads she reaches for quill and ink; her diary. For this moment she does not cry, nor even complain, in a way it is her sanity, she writes perhaps the price of flour, or how the blacks have disappeared; maybe Dan is away, in London, Sydney, Melbourne, north, south, east, west; secretly she enjoys the challenge of the landscape, the loneliness, the work — she must have. And if she could not write she could spin a yarn — never was she as mad as the shepherd who talked to his hat. Because it would not be fair to

---

The book reviewed in this article is: Kate Jennings, ed., *Mother I'm Rooted* (Outback Press, Melbourne, 1975).

Dan, or to Tommy or to little Harriet, she never attempts the suicide she often contemplates . . . But at times, in places, she whines and whinges, becomes the neurotic housewife who only wants to go home to England, to go back to the oak-panelling in the study of the paternal household where Daddy puffed his pipe and wanted the best for her. Thought of Mother cools her down, she turns to her husband whom she has chosen wherever he may go, whatever he may be . . .

> (Duty bound
> for home
> and love
> and life
> she set off
> with a man
> who'd rescued her
> from home
> and love
> and life —
> at home . . .¹)

If she is 'gentle', here there is no time for her quaint accomplishment with piano and water colour. Needle, yes; but save the fancy work for a christening gown. The pen? (Am I wrong?) Or is it possible Australian women were writers from the start? Am I wrong to guess about the lonely talent burning oil at the kitchen table? Names spring to mind — to yours too — I will not mention any of them; and into my own ancestry I can remember — is it memory? — my great-grandmother making money out of pubs after the gold rushes — two weak husbands I think she had — and losing it in the '90s. The '90s, when men were making legends sentimentally out of a time already past.

Allow me to continue in an illogical, wandering, emotional, 'feminine' way, in other words, don't ask me to *prove* what I know one way or another: this is not a masculine country. Look at the shape of Ayer's Rock, the Olgas, the gum tree, our hills — it lacks the phallic thrust of those gothic snow trees and mountain peaks of Northern Europe. Europe: Western Christian seed-thrower, imperialist, expansionist, capitalist, God-made-man, man-made-God, almighty dictator of lifestyle — man, wife and child style . . .

But I have wandered from the diary by the kerosene lamp — my crochet is haywire and full of loose ends. Who would have believed it? A thick book full of women poets, and for each one of the 152 women[2] published I would bet on at least six more at kitchen tables. Women may smile. Here and there a man might ask why? does this mean anything? should I care?

Flipping through *Mother I'm Rooted:* wives angry at their husbands' right of possession . . . 'I woke to your harsh probing fingers . . . I in anger escaped you' ('Of Necessity', Barbara Giles, 1963); woman tortured by the man and his son, 'The man is oedipal, the son ejaculates prematurely' ('The Shape of Belief', Wilma Hedley, 223); 'women who despise women must live in fear of mirrors', a plea to male-identified women 'torn twixt prostitute and saint on journeys that start and end in limbo' (Jill Miller, 373); women speaking of their unimportance, of their strangeness to themselves, of being vegetable to be eaten (Marjorie Pizer, 429; Debbie Penny, 425); women reassessing the romance of motherhood and childbirth, 'But you end up owing that baby twenty years' love and security' (Penelope Nelson, 397); women taking a straight look at their lovers . . . 'wondering if next time I replaced myself with a mirror would he really mind?' ('Thoughts', Angela Catterns, 100); women wanting release from the 'awkward meteorite of affection' (Margaret Henry, 235); women trapped in definitions, 'I am not/that which you think I am . . . do not make me be/that which, I think/you think I am/for I am never that/learn me anew/every moment/or know me not at all' (Lynmore Dover, 142); liberated women mistaken for libertine women (G. Laurence, 321); daughters in rebellion against mothers' tyranny . . . 'old nappies/ (rags, she called them)/no I yelled/I didn't need her/help/to get one on' ('Swamp Song', Lorna, 324). And finally those (like Margot Nash, 390) who

>   want to say
>   that this time it's my turn
>   to remain intact.
>   And this time,
>   whatever we build together,
>   if we do,
>   will be on my terms too.

Poetry and communication? Poetry as communication — as telephone, life-line, telegram, banging at the door — holding us with its glittering eye ... (we cannot but choose to hear). The book bears reading from the first page to the last. The poets are grouped alphabetically. Themes recur, images recur. Reading thus, one gets the sense of a huge female being, threatening, energetic, suddenly articulate, moving, clumsily and embarrassingly and courageously, and with moments of superb grace. Not permitted the self-indulgences of recent decorative mannerism, nor naturally in tune with the concept of poem *as objet d'art,* twisted by trying to please male personalities in editorial positions, finding themselves at a loss, women who write poetry have been forced to look at the lowest common denominator — communication. Into the strict metrical patterns of the '50s they tried to fit, but their words were luscious and their rhythms jangly — they tried to fit into a copied mould; they failed. They sounded phoney and trivial. The re-emergence of feminism, the general ease encouraged by the peace and love generation, and the influence of American poets, perhaps specifically the New York School — Frank O'Hara, Ted Berrigan, Anne Waldron — which said *anything* is the subject of poetry, plus other developments of the last few years, must have caused women individually to question the validity of the standards they were trying to reach. Realising that these were false, that *obedience* was irrelevant, that there is no right and wrong, they were left with their simple need. Out of their need to say comes a new style, with rhythms of urgency, passion, pain, anger ... bald rhythms, harsh words. Defensiveness. Attack. Outback Press gives us a publication which marks the advent of a new Australian women's poetry, a new phenomenon on the literary scene.

Kate Jennings says in her Introduction that *Mother I'm Rooted*

> became a collective statement about the position of women in Australia. It also became, on my part, an attempt to question the standards of what is supposed to be good and bad poetry in the prevailing literary hegemony ... I think the women in the book ... write because they need and want to express themselves, and they have something to say, in their own voices. No oughts.

Kate Jennings opened a space, cleared the floor of preconceptions, definitions, objective rules, advertised widely, was inundated with poems and chose 'mainly on the grounds of women writing directly, and honestly'. The political and social climate, as well as personal conflicts and crisis of identity, is forcing women to ask themselves questions revolutionaries usually ask: meaning? reasons? what can be changed? what must be changed? how? The beauty of such questions is that they force a quest for answers, or for some solution, albeit a personal solution — the asking destroys complacency, comfort, laziness, acceptance of the status quo.

The book is interesting to read on any page, but now and then I am struck by the strength of a verse, and not only by what it is saying but how it is done. Sylvia Kantarizis has a sure control over her social-realist subject matter, a sense of line and of the effect of simple accurate words. Kerryn Higgs uses a contemplative lyrical style to gaze steadily at herself and her life, and throughout the thirteen pages of her poetry it is evident that she considers herself a representative member of a generation which must change the world. It is fascinating work. Chris Sitka is an eloquent poet with a message and uncompromising dedication; for this she juxtaposes exotic images like hot lava flowing from her eyes with actual occurrences anywhere in the world to horrifying effect. Helen Bansemer hits nails on their heads crisply and quickly.

It seems unfair to single out particular poets when it is such a large anthology. The editorial hand is evident; Kate Jennings has a taste for a female poetry which reflects the experiences of women who are actively investigating their own reality. Much of the work is trite and doggerel, not at all notable except for the fact that the doggerel is about subjects previously unmentionable; good taste found, for instance, menstruation difficult. A familiar humour helps to excuse those which tend to be distasteful. Some of the work is straight humour — women laughing at themselves in verse is a welcome change from the prevailing earnestness which begins to be trying. On the gentle note is Margaret Nossiter's 'Lament of Wife and Mother', a poem which stops me in my tracks, as if indeed I had found my own grandmother's diary and was standing, reading, helplessly remarking what an uncommonly pleasant turn of phrase she had. Its simple sincerity is couched in easy metre and rhyme. There is a peculiar mixing of old-fashioned styles with crude innovations in the techniques occurring throughout the book — a polarity which suggests that this is the first step towards a new feminine poetic genre. This first step being to do, to be honest and to risk failure. The next step will be to look into the failures and successes, and then to risk failure again by reaching out from the successes towards a satisfactory form which will be able to express the deep changes women are experiencing, the inventive thought and reassessment of basic principles that these changes demand.

She has a good mind with which she is contemplating the water — there seems no way out but in: she is given no reason for living but him, but for him other things are more important than she — she will take herself right off his stage, give him room to complete his mission, both out of love for him and stinging with the insults he has dealt, thoughtlessly. 'Good*bye*, Prince Hamlet.' *Mother I'm Rooted* is a feminist book.[4] Phyllis Chesler in *Women and Madness* advances the thesis that society allows so little right for women to be themselves, to think for themselves, to respond with truth to themselves that often they retreat into madness: but that madness is male-defined — it is madness not to accept happily the role of wife and mother (conversely, it is madness to aim for such a role as it is dependent on other individuals — husband and children — who may or may not be wonderful, but the odds are against a fulfilled life since the woman's achievement is constantly limited) — furthermore, prevailing psychotherapy is designed to educate or force women into the submissive, nurturant mould. *In the interests of family integrity.* The family has an unequal power distribution which makes not only for individual neurosis, but for widespread cultural neurosis.[5] All 152 poets on each of the 500 pages of *Mother I'm Rooted* are lighting up small and large sections of the unsatisfactory walls which surround us. Some see cracks, some see solid steel, some assess the work of chipping away they've already started, some curl up in misery, some daydream, sing 'hey non nonny, nonny, hey nonny.' I need not name the women writers of this century who have chosen suicide — undoubtedly their intelligence and sensibility made them aware of the enormity of what was against them. As Simone de Beauvoir says, 'Representation of the world, like the world itself, is the work of men; they describe it from their own point of view, which they confuse with absolute truth.'[6]

The difficulty in attempting any sort of analysis of cultural development in Australia lies in the insidious as well as the obvious effect of imports we receive from older cultures. I do not deny that continual and changing immigration is one of the central aspects of the character of Australia. But Australia is a younger nation, and all Australians have a short literary history, and women are not greatly out-numbered by men in their contribution. Our women are not so far from their hardy forebears. Australian women are in the peculiar position of having not only new territories in the women's predicament to explore, but also a nation which by its nature is both vulnerable to and patently in need of experiment in and a maturation of its existing cultural assumptions and foundations. Women are not naturally weak, and as they are now facing the challenge of literature, they will bring strength and depth to the field. *Mother I'm Rooted* is a beginning: out into the light of day valuable scribblings have come which might otherwise have only had the midnight lamp, the dusty drawer, the eyes of an idle grand-daughter . . .

> hopefully this book will provoke a debate about 'standards'. I don't know any longer what is 'good' and what is 'bad'. I have been trained to know, in a patriarchal university, on a diet of male writers. We have to go back to bedrock, and explore thoroughly that which is female and that which is male, and then perhaps we can approach androgyny, and humanity.[7]

There is more than suicide and madness; a new stage is being built.

Notes

1 Helen Bansemer, *Mother I'm Rooted*, p. 29
2 Of the 152 names, four I believe are men. Helen Bansemer is not one of them; a man wouldn't/couldn't come up with what she is saying. She writes a feminine *reality* and her words ring with consequent *truth*.
3 All page numbers are from *Mother I'm Rooted*, Outback Press, Melbourne, 1975.
4 'The motivation behind this book is feminist. I'm using the word feminist in its broadest sense. "Feminism is simply a belief in the full humanity of woman and her right to define herself." (see the admirable introduction to *Rising Tides,* anthology of American women's poetry).' Kate Jennings, *Mother I'm Rooted,* Introduction.
5 Shulamith Firestone, *The Dialectic of Sex,* London, 1972, p. 63
6 Quoted in Firestone, *ibid,* p. 148
7 Kate Jennings, *op cit,* Introduction

Sketches

First

An abstract pattern struck me at a designated
   point in my existence:
the skeleton of a leaf/ A
particular leaf at a particular place in a particular moment
When
I saw that all Nature had skeletal balance
   of a higher order than
the equality of symmetry.
I saw
myself at a point on the graph of my own existence.
The point: the realisation/ a
bisection in the pattern of comprehension
   which diagrams my mind
as simply as integral a part of the scheme of things
as the mesh of a skeleton leaf.

As simply.

Detail One
The coincidence is no coincidence
and so on.

In another substance, my life spanning time and place,
  my growth until
my end, may even be graphed in similar proportions
  to my body
described two dimensionally.
As once, in conversation, I learnt
of fish
drawn on an x-y scale become,
according to the ratio of x:y,
drawings of separate species of fish,
exactly.

Detail Two
The palm of my hand,
the arrangement and relationship to each other
  of the planets
segmented from the pinpoint of the time and
  place of my birth,
the changing ageing of my face,
the design of my emotional and mental energy
must each
have the imprint of my uniqueness
(same as
the snow crystal
the leaf).

Second

The East wind
travelling faster than the earth
troubles
so
the need to create
disturbs.

It disturbs,
in gusts.

Third

Language being the matter of literature
plans and passion
having no less a place
along the chorus line
understates itself
with excellence.

Pity the soloist,
restless &
temperamental/
Bearing the load
of light.

Screams From A Primal Quarter

Trees hung upside down from the sky
attached to star points in that blue earth
because there were no clouds
not then
there was a moon reflecting
the sea, miles from beaches
where brown bodies have drowned —
some brown foot was taken by a shark,
a shark who had discovered more
than wild hunger.

The surfer returned on a belly board.

The sun-sea threw blue light into the moon.
And the road's dotted line
swung west of my wheels, and,
in drug rhythm, flowed
back east of my wheels.
   Yes, I am driving through my life.
   You laugh. But dawn has not yet come.
The teeth of people — and, incidentally, shark's teeth,
can be cruel —
when they discover more than wild hunger.

I never took for some pure reason.
I never took for a wild hungry purpose.

'Don't laugh. Don't ridicule me,
because I turned my world inside out!'

I see your carefree white surf
grinning, and your board slides over my head,
I see it all —
the malicious happy freedom,
but I don't know you —
I don't care to know you —
to find out your secrets —
the jaws in my face open out
and I snap.
Your foot, fine surfer, is mine!

The boy returned on a belly board.

And the road is a hollow tube
containing me and
my motion like spinning makes a gravity
not real — or
not of the world and its sun —
so the dotted line swings
west and east
and ties me up.
In knots.

I scream: Don't laugh at me!
The human thongs in knots
in tangles, picking at itself
Don't open your bubbling froth —
don't show your whiteness —
at my crude ways.
The road in the night —
in the early naked hours —
is a puzzle-ring.
And I can't work it out.

Frenzy. Impatience. Anger.
And repression.

The surfer. Yes. The one-footed surfer,
he goes on the sea. And
that, the belly board, goes
here
between him and the
sea.
The upside down
trees?
   The tube?
      The ribbon-drunken road
turning me
   its annoying fly
away from its eyes —
   the eyes of the road?

Please don't laugh — I promise
to take the trees from the stars
and return them to their roots —
and the footless boy — with courage —
to ocean with a board.

I will hurl my slip-knot to the moon
and this —
as I am not anchored —
will suspend me.

But dawn has not yet come.

Bella

Bella you are a candle in me
in a low roped-off corner — dark —
which I tried to hide — dust
is there now — but once —
ah once! Light was everywhere,
warm near that queer fire
under the stair, cunning charm,
quiet desire. Bella bella bella
fear. I was like that then.
You flicker a rusty flame — low
and cool — cramped — dirty
dust in the damp and past.
Bella I'll keep you from the draught.

Prose Looks At Photographs

1
Four rectangles are set up. Targets. Sculptures on a lawn.
Faces and shoulders. Expressions caught
   in impossible stillness.
The yellow table has a different stillness.

2
Photos are always past. Glass reflects the moving present.
Now that the eye moves.
An eye aches at the base of my spine, this family is mine.
The nutrient that constipates, and hides
   curatives in cupboards
with cups. Family afraid of bodies, easy to verbalize the
natural law, and argue. Shout at targets on the lawn.
Iron- plated with
time, small specklings of patina. The green in the
room is an empty bottle of scotch. Ice locks away the silly
minute.

3
Snap.
'Eat like a poor man. Look at your cheese mournfully.'

4
Three women and a boy. One is me. One is dead. One
is a boy no longer. The one without frame is propped
beside grapes and golden Chrysanthemums. Long lasting
flowers. Caught in cold imitation of what a family was,
sisters and brothers, games and dares . . .
   the memory-fiction
of a private tableau in a life somehow lived, scientifically

lived — there must have been days, meals,
   biological change,
laughter forgotten — the fact is the present moves and the
past is frozen isolation. A second in a lens compressing,
pretending to contain, the millions
   not photographed, complete.
Indeed complete enough. The eye which sees
will always move.

5

Away. To. Back. On. Adding and subtracting
   its own occurrences.
Give me sex. Give me what should have but did not . . .
   Dry ice
smoke shush this is sacred, the family.
   Patina is sorely bought,
lies with aid understanding. Lend romance to fiction.
   But the
parkland not the workshop. Make that the greenroom;
   the lawn a
stage — whichever way the tableau suits.
   Choose yellows and blue.
Spinnakers on yachts in the sun.

6

Build up a Saturday afternoon into a prose painting,
   practise
the art and craft of it. Have a still winter image,
   four bronze
sculptures in the rain and saturated green.
   Come colourful in
your raincoats and anoraks with the wind
   tearing ice-drops from
your noses and ear lobes and walk casually
   complainingly between
the trees and these. Stare at the eye holes,
   and I ask, see blue
and gold in the never ending twinkle of the sea.

7
'Though we are poor let us eat fillet mignon
  and creamed potatoes.
Though we do eat at the tired kitchen table,
  please wear shoes and
look presentable at dinner. Do not start
  until the last is served
and hold your knife this way. Pretend you are not
  starving.
Always leave a little on your plate when you have finished.
  Small
signs will make life easier later.'

8
My brother. Good. Handsome. Neat. Straight honest look.
I cannot see this photograph without the myths
  of his great
schoolboy career.
Now I see shrewdness.
Now I don't. It questions.
Now it's tired.
Now sad.
Now humour
Now very intelligent.
Now knowing me.
Now indifferent.
The other eye is calm. Seems to ride the large nose like a
yachtsman a yacht.
A technically competent portrait. My grandmother
  must have
been there to take care of the collar and tie perfection.
Suddenly he reminds me of a boy I know,
  and that gives me a
faint air of exploitativeness. Now the power,
  the confidence
of masculinity sitting on an education and a civilisation.
I am surprised at what these short sharp looks
  have taught me.

9
But the eye of the present moves and teaches.
A steel stare contradicts a glance of amusement:
Was he then a leader?

10
I do not look into the lens of the camera. I squat plucking
leaves. The sun shines through my transparent fingernails.

11
Photos of my sister were collected
 the day after she died, and
the best was blown up to make a portrait
 for everybody. Therefore
the secret of colour photography, the little dots,
 are evident as
she squints towards the camera in the sunshine.
 She smiles.

12
My other sister grins at something beyond
 the right shoulder of
the photographer. Clear-cut. Clean.

13
Drawing the thirteenth rectangle twice. Death.
    Tarot targets,
and the question, is the future frozen expectation?
    Will there
be books or sculptures on the lawn? I prefer
    a lively gallery
with the challenge of art within the frames —
    that's why the
individual eye now darts and stares.
    Flickers and twinkles in
the stare.
The steps and stairs of a catholic girlhood
    leave me now practising
prose. In a suit of cards. Make it hearts
    to match an open fire
and games of bridge I never won.
My brother, the cook, the leader, the teacher . . .
In another room a glass statue of Don Quixote
    stands erect beside
a bowl of Narcissus.

The Room With A Mirror

The mirror, a large one, opens this other person's room like a book at a pictorial centre-fold, offering to the imagination no more than hints of what has been before and will come after. One cannot help guessing. Waiting. The mirror at an oblique angle to the couch shows the more distant perspective reaching as it does out the window and into the street where tiny figures move unconscious of being seen, anonymous as ants. The buildings, road, occasional human beings and the fluid motion of automobiles are curtailed in one corner of the page by a painter's rule of the window-frame and the edge of the mirror, denoting a definite contrast of mood and light.

The room is still as gloom and predominantly brown with the greens and ochres of the floralesque patterns on the mats and armchairs of a generation or two ago. Dust moves as a silent regular snoop which when discovered panics in a swirling billow of lies and guilt wishing to hide again at the soonest opportunity. Insidious guest. Depressing thoughts are mapped across the walls where on the parchment-paint age designs its direct routes, watermarks the rivers, smokestains the forests, and traces the tracks of time passing on the inside; inside a single room of an erection built in the 1930s for the accommodation of bachelors who work in the city by day. By year the bachelors and single girls come and go leaving their landmarks on the map, their droppings on the carpet and the breath of stale nights in the corners.

The time past in here is not venerable. This age is material and dull as if the time merely peeled off layer by layer the lustres of the present.

The mirror dominates the wall facing the door on to the outside world. Unsuitably modern in its simple square expanse and the gloss finish given to the light and objects reflected there, the glass calls interest into its own dimension. One is reminded of the famous looking glass and other fantasies, so abrupt is the contrast of texture and suggestion. The yellow gloom of the room looks attractive in there, a careful glow devised by a film director to give such a place a quality of drama and suspense, a hush before an entrance. Into the lulls of reality dreams of marvellous fiction flow rushing like air into a vacuum. What legendary mixture of great actress and great character combined will enter and proclaim: 'What a dump!'? One cannot tolerate empty suspension of actual emotion and therefore hunts the imagination for a slim-legged Crawford to enter knocking over the vase of dying flowers, tearing down the rice-paper lantern, brutally kicking away the paperbacks which tumble out of a bookcase in the hallway and staring with disgust down at the red remains of spaghetti on a blue willow-patterned plate. Behind the magnificent face, and because of it, the dismal background pulses imperceptibly with a drama that will be set up, suffered and complete within the tiny flight of the spectator emotion.

Silence, the dream dries us for want of belief. Not quiet, it is that silence of no one and nothing to do but wait. Waiting, eyes unfocused, outstretched hand tapping the hide of the couch, dust rising as if it were a horse being patted. Where is the hay? The texture of the room returns. A pinpoint veil of dust rests, even over the mirror. This lifeless piece of glass shows the shut front door and the grey suburban street — melancholy grey of deep dust.

The short story is like a painting in a frame. It depicts, it pleases, it has a single light source. A short story has a single point to make and everything mentioned in it is lit from this angle. Within this strict, universal necessity the form is as flexible as colour in shaped space.

Prose in the case of story writing, has the important component of humanity. Perhaps doing it arises from a psycho-emotional need in the writer to wring out soggy bits of the self, or perhaps what she wrings out is the paint or the colour which gives light or depth to a subject matter that is not actually herself.

I have tried to write stories which face a blackness in my emotional experience. We do not in the end include these stories in this collection, a yuckiness spills across the page. I do not understand. It is not me. It is me. There is ignorance. Amnesia. Men having this disturbance have looked up and out and cast the blame or the nobility on to the feminine Muse. They have hurled the wretched inner ignorance away and spent it on something they can never know from inside, hence can invent into whatever.

Doris Lessing said in her interview with Virginia Fraser that the memory blots the really terrible things out. I feel the steel trapdoors, like concussion, over parts of my biography in my own head. But what is happening in those sewers — those necessary, grubby drains — and how much can they bear? How much turning against oneself can a woman take? How much shit put on her from outside can she dispose of in her own psyche?

Writers depend to a great extent on psychological plumbing. We must keep the maintenance up and the way of the flow clear. Many of us turn much of that shit into good mulch and compost and grow works of art and fiction with strong roots and healthy leaves. In Search Of Our Mothers' Garden *is a marvellous title, used well by Alice Walker.*

In the first of 'The Illusive Quality Stories', the poet-coward is the classic scribe in the corner preserving his head by being nice to everyone, especially the reigning dictator. This is the nature of fiction writers, they live to tell the tales.

It is mightily unfair that women who have this peculiar ironic talent also have to be heroines. In some senses it does take heroic proportions to go on digging one's own depths to make literature, while keeping house, feeding others, fighting oppression and nuclear destruction, struggling to hold faith in one's own work.

Flaubert said, art alone gives life value. He rejected closeness with his mistress to make her into his Muse, unabashedly. We are our own Muse it seems. The masculine spirit has not become generous enough yet to give itself so selflessly for others' inspiration.

But we have fruits from the male tree. We have inherited their forms. We have read much more men's work than we have women's. They have given us the lengthy classics, the great tragedies and a million stories. Writers of both sexes are within this tradition. It's as impossible to do away with a good story as it is to do away with painting in a frame.

Black, Silver And Grey

She was amazed at the hardness of his body, his muscles. Men have hard bodies. The softness of her thighs against the wound cables of muscle down his legs rendered her defenceless. She knew this. She was as light as a feather.

She wondered about the meaning, and the sincerity of her senses. Were they, anyway, responding? Should her mind wander? The stars were out. Romance is in the stars.

Drowned in her childhood was the conviction of romance. A conviction woven by experience when the moon was tossed light upon a rocky sea and, frightened and cold, she threw her romance up into the soft silver and black sky. She hemmed her life with this knowledge, the infinite possibilities of romance. Romance was simply a feeling then, not even a word.

The man was a stranger when he opened his eyes. His words were rock, what's wrong? Confused by his concern that he was not pleasing her, he slumped head in hands into instant depression. Nothing! Nothing's wrong. The future without him was a morbid prospect.

She had to give in, swallow the pride of her unattainable black and silver skies. There was caress and comfort in her touch, and she lifted his face to hers. The smile in her eyes was flooded with warmth and humility. The woman had swallowed a secret pride, sacrificed it on the altar of man's ever-important present. Reciprocally, his pride swung high again. She was carried along on the tide of his energy.

Her own warmth and humility seeped into her own blood stream, thrilled her. Her smile was her emotion, warm, energetic and giving. Oh to give without counting the cost. But to give all was to give the cost as well. At this moment, there was only immersion.

He looked at his watch, 'Good Lord. I don't want to leave, but there are other things, my job, my responsibility to sleep.' She had no idea of the time.

Her eyes were closed, hiding her jealous protection of the calm comfortable emotion, as if the sky was a still beauty like that of a Grecian urn. Cunningly she nestled into him not to move, begging him not to move an inch.

He left. Both smiled to themselves.

Three Men In A Boat

'We're going to fall in,' said one of the men.
Three men sat in a broad-beamed boat. There were no holes in the hull, nor was there a dangerous listing to one side. The boat was on a lake, and the lake was calm; there were no ripples, save the circles feathering out in the wake of a family of ducks.

'We're going to fall in,' one of the men said.
He clasped the firmly made willow-wood seat with both hands until eight knuckle joints were white, and sat tensely in the centre of the stern. His eyes hard with panic, stared dead ahead, glued, as it were, to fear. The sky was a bird's egg blue on the horizon, and the blue overhead bore no arguing with; nor did it cause argument, for those who would argue didn't look up and these who looked up accepted and suffered no crick in the neck. The hills in the distance, so serenely solid, expressed no heaviness; their colour was purple. Yet the near hills were yellow as hay and thick-set as a Dutch peasant girl.

'We're going to fall in,' he repeated.
And near the shores of the lake, to the west, and on the starboard side of the bow, six weeping willow trees hid their sturdy trunks and branches behind a curtain of down-turning leaves, the lowest of which dipped lightly into the surface of the lake, and in such a multitude of lime-green, light-loving foliage, no leaf stirred. For this moment, anyway, not even a tired one chose to detach itself and rock nonchalantly, gravity-bound, to the still water. To the east on the port side of the clinkerbuilt boat, the lake shallowed to allow reeds to grow, and in the silence if your ears were finely tuned you could hear only the gentle sounds of a pair of wading birds sleeping somewhere in the density of growth. Beneath the birds, in the

cool mud, minute life carried on as usual, but this was as invisible to human comprehension as is the chaotic activity within the neutron of an atom.

'We're going to fall in,' he said again into what seemed to him the devastatingly empty space over the lake.

'What's got into you?' said the mate of his who held the oars. His rowing was becoming increasingly incompetent as the fear of his friend gained profundity through repeated expression in the maddeningly gentle silence all around. He had been staring at the dipping of his left oar and it had dawned on him how deep was the still water underneath and how little the oar penetrated.

'Shut up!' commanded the one in the front.
He was scowling, his eyebrows were down, narrow eyes as narrow as possible and his top lip was up. He was pinching his face into a point and turning it around left to right, right to left; his blunt forefinger tapped the weapon on his lap.

The tension in the boat resembled that within a man, who at the age of thirty-eight has still some way to go in the pursuing of his career and with the payments on the house, etc., who is in the waiting room immediately before his second visit to the specialist, and his question (rolling roudily around his mind like the engine of an electric train set on a simple circular track) is: what are the results of the tests? Do I have it? His mind at this point of tension has taken over his whole being with its manic impatience and moronic repetition to such an extent that he doesn't even trust gravity; he feels it is possible that the whole solid mass of the city, his world, and the suburbs, his home, and the country, his block of land and tax-evasion scheme, will crumble about him, and he will be alone, weightless, dead in the nothingness — the poor cells in his body are crushed together with all the strength of his clenched fists and are like poor sheep pushed and piled on top of one another in a cattle truck bumping along a rutted road at 100 kph. The tension in the hired boat contrasted with the busy but thoroughly peaceful work of the animal, vegetable, insect and chemical community on the bottom of the lake, some thirty feet below.

'Christ, it's deep here!' said the one with the oars.

'No, it isn't, it's just dirty,' said the one with the gun.

'We're going to fall in,' pronounced the other. This time with all the thundering import and impressive impact and temporary success of the Prophet of Doom. He began to shudder.

The birds were not singing at this time of day in the trees by the shore, and made no noise except for tiny domestic arguments in their nests so well camouflaged in the brush and bush as to be rarely seen. But the men were too deaf to overhear these delightful little fights.

It was the last time he said it, for on hearing him shake the cosmos with such terror-filled and terrible words the family of ducks took flight. The flapping of the wings of the seven of them and the splashing of the water as they lifted out their webbed feet and slapped them into the surface of the lake created the intensity of noise usually associated with 'take-off' and frightened the hell out of the three men in the boat, and each began praying in his own way.

The one in the bow stood up, blaspheming to the forgotten Christianity of his parents and overbalanced. As his weight was shattering the calm surface of the lake and the sudden loss of it was making the boat rock dangerously, the oarsman pressed all his weight down on the handles, murmuring 'Holy Mother of God Jesus Mary . . .', in a vain and irrational effort to cease relationship with the still depths he had been trying to negotiate with inexpert rowing and projection of blame on to the water he feared. The waving of the oars in the air contributed to the perilous rocking, so much so that over the left side slipped a slosh of water which rapidly made its way past the esky, the sleeping bags, the heavy knapsack of tinned baked beans and through a collection of woollen pullovers to the right side, which, with all the vigour of a right-hander's punch, threw back a bigger and faster quantity of water. The 'prophet' himself performed a calisthenic feat his ego would have loved to have shown at the gym: his already tired hands and arms lifted his whole body off the seat, his feet shot forward knocking his mate with the oars on to his back, where he rolled groaning, his knees to his chest, and in the midst of his groan on the left he injested a mouthful of lake water and began painfully coughing, spluttering and choking. The other came out of his isometrics with a thump that cracked his coccyx bone; he then dissolved into tears of guilt and agony.

'Hell — damn — what's going on?' he yelled.

Gradually the boat stopped rocking, but it had taken water up to the level of the seats and was quickly sinking. The fellow sitting on the floor near the bow had realised the lake was fresh water and swallowed away the last of his cough and was trying to remove his waterlogged clothes in preparation for a swim.

'Don't move, you idiot!' ordered the 'prophet'.

'We're sinking anyway, you mug.'

'I can't swim, I've broken a bone I think,' he said vaguely. 'Where's Mack?' he asked, staring hopelessly at the now stilling water of the lake.

'Food for fish,' replied the other, before he splashed heavily into the lake, causing the boat to rock first, then, capsize over the aft, taking the frightened moaner by surprise to his prompt death.

All the poor man's lies came home to him, now. He had told his mates he could swim so often he had forgotten to remind himself of the truth that he couldn't. But he wouldn't have had mates if he'd told what really was, what he really was, what really happened, he had reasoned so many times. Now his boringly ordinary self was drowning slowly and he was surprised at his own inner distance from these pointlessly flapping arms, those feet down there pedalling of their own accord. This indifference is wrong, he thought as he went down feet first with his eyes open. A foot or so down it became darker, yet he could see a little. His eyes were wide with amazement at the fact that he was surviving without breath for so long, and then his feet hit the bottom. He believed at that moment, a half second, that he still had the choice: to remove his clothes, kick up to the surface, the air, and swim to the shore — that one where the reeds were. If he had not chosen to attempt to do that, he would have seen what too few have the privilege to see — daily life at the bottom of the lake — but he, instead, created murky clouds of mud and panic among the indigenes as he desperately used up his last ounce of strength, and became a dead thing floating in the gravity-less environment of water.

A late afternoon breeze had sprung up, flicking the various species of birds into action and song; the hay on the hills began to sway and the purple of the distant ones became deeper as heavier clouds gathered over the north horizon; and on the now quite choppy surface of the lake the upturned hull of the clinkerbuilt row-boat bobbed about, making a slow journey to the curtain of weeping willow leaves and to hide next to its living cousins, the trunks and branches there.

A Nightmare Leads To A Scandal

Frances forgets nothing. Once a toddler taught herself remembergames to alleviate loneliness in a large family.

Nightly between lights-out and sleep, Frances recalled every detail of the boarding-school day: all the facts of history and geography, biology and chemistry, French verbs, a look exchanged in the corridor, a smell issuing from another girl, the taste of a vegetable, a new way of balancing for a backhand: while her forefinger gently caressed her clitoris. She compressed the day's details into pockets, stuffing her mind so full it had to burst. And burst it would with the small orgasm of masturbation. In that moment of great tension and its flowing release, the knowing of her body and the learning of her mind coalesced in a confusion and enlightenment which confounded all ladders of logic. It gave Frances a hard-earned yet short-lived peace, for sheer exhaustion tossed her on her right side and she slept like a heavy log on her narrow mattress.

Then the unconscious, uncontrolled state where the trained and tamed mind, finally having broken its chains and taken off into primitive regions of violent colour and ferocious honesty, would make catastrophes, tragedies and hideous monsters come at her. Poor Frances was dragged into situations which overwhelmed her and left her to the mercy of her pitiless fears. This night, searing pain in her uterus woke her, and the bed was damp. At the window she saw the moon as a scimitar and the stars and planets bits and pieces of the pure white body it had destroyed in a passionate rage, and the blank navy-blue sky the forensic blanket on which it was all being examined. Looking up at the sky, Frances saw herself as eternally fragmented. Her horror froze her body into splinters of ice.

Shivering by the dormitory window, she tried to know more, to bring it down to her mental understanding. Yet all her talents were paralysed. She couldn't even know whether to fetch her dressing-gown or move her weight from her left foot to her right. The problem stopped all that. Her mind grasped: 'If I cannot be both man and woman, I must be in some sense always a victim. Deep in the foetus, deep in the genes . . . vic vic victim. Might as well jump.'

She scratched the window pane, but she did not try to act, all her courage was spent in considering, and her energy in shivering. The practical terror of knowing her bed was no friend, and the question of the wetness, 'is it just perspiration?', brought out a tremble. 'Perhaps I urinated?' Cold fast tears ran into the corner of her mouth.

Sophie counted the minutes. Unlike Frances she was a light sleeper, but a generally untroubled one. Sophie counted the minutes since she was woken by Frances's muffled sounds of sleep-bound terror. She had given herself a waiting, listening time of fifteen minutes, because her desire to comfort was ambiguous, and the expectation exciting. As she stared at her fluorescent watch, she vaguely went over their differences. Frances was athletic and brainy, serious and withdrawn, she liked Bartok and Shostakovich. She topped the class in music theory. While she, Sophie, was fat, played the saxophone by ear, listened to New Orleans jazz exclusively and did the easiest subjects. Even if she was to be disappointed and not able to put her ample arms about that long, intelligent head and press it into her breasts, the waiting time was delicious.

She had heard her neighbour get out of bed, heard the stumbling footsteps, heard the scraping of the glass, and then she had heard complete hush for six whole minutes, until that tremble escaped, followed by the sniffle.

At that, Sophie could contain her friendliness no longer.

Nothing else could have saved Frances that night. The girls made love until dawn. By mass, at seven thirty, they were in love. The bloody sheets where Frances had haemorrhaged, having broken her own hymen in the grip of the witches of sleep, were happily dealt with by Sophie, who did not suffer the crippling shyness of Frances and longed now to serve. She liked skipping the odd class. During mass, both were preoccupied with the thought of each other. From not even being friends, they were lovers. Not buddies before because Frances, the scholarship student, was suspicious of Sophie, the daughter of wealth, Sophie who escaped Phys. Ed. to play her saxophone, Sophie who could use either her charm or the privilege of her family background to do what she chose, Sophie, the popular. Now as they filed up to communion, Frances felt all her suspicions melt before the glorious beauty she had discovered in this fat, lazy, spoilt brat who was sneekily touching her hand.

Before her affair with Frances, Sophie had taken many girls into her bed in her now long boarding school career, with gentle affection and innocent animal warmth, their ignorance of sexual finesse saving them from the horrors of sin. She was well practised in the deceptions needed for the 'let's be friends' customs of the girls and dissembled cheerfully and successfully for the months of secret passion which roughly spanned the distance from her birthday, on 10th of May to Frances's on 18th of November. Six months of bliss. Sophie's wonderful voice rang out in the chapel with lusty holiness, her comfortably large body and long fair wrinkly hair matched the blue veil of the Children of Mary, her prefect's badge was like an insignia of authority rightly hers through the virtue of her popularity with both nuns and pupils, she exuded an impression of overall goodness. Sophie did have a manifest spirituality, she was sincere in her kindness to others and her great lungs enabled her to give praise to the godhead in the finest way devised by Christianity, through the hymn, so her love of singing compounded in her intuitive mind with her love of god, or Life, or It. The sunshine. Theological analysis did not trouble her. Whatever faith was, she had it, obviously.

In these months her love of Frances was of the same essence, except for the merely social, necessary lies. Happy with a righteous self-deception, she fucked Frances with a passion that equalled her friend's.

There was never such innocence or ignorance possible for Frances. She had discovered her nervy, pleasure centres before she learnt the alphabet. She was born with a respect for the importance of her body and hence for the huge intelligence of matter. Her love for Sophie was a vital link in understanding their connection. Her love was her attachment to nature, her merging with it, her comprehension and experience of true beauty. Real, palpable beauty. The pinnacle. She hated the authority of boarding school even more, now, for its injustice, its wrongness, in proclaiming what she knew to be the finest thing in life to be a vice, a sin. Her hate was a smouldering rage which in her dimensions was as deep as Lucifer's jealousy in his. The fusion of love, of sexual experiment and expansion, and her decision not to fritter away such knowledge in useless daydreaming and sentimental fantasies with the hostility of the surrounding environment, the necessity of secrecy and deception and the consequent fear brought her to strong religious convictions. Defined by the nuns' R.K. classes, her intellect came to a philosophy of the necessity of the Devil. The Devil was the definer, the separator, the father of humanity. The Fall was a fall away from androgyny, a fall away into two, or multiple parts, as a single pail of water falls into many drops, yet remains water. She began to understand the male and female sexuality within herself, whole experience was possible no matter what the gender of the partner. The real sexual difference was that between making love with someone and masturbating.

One night when the moon was fat and incomplete near the end of the year, a fresh-faced young postulant was nervously checking on the dormitories after lights-out. This young lady had brought from her sheltered home a noctophobia of pathological proportions. The spooky rounds were a part of her training. Her novice mistress had hinted to her that a certain amount of sleeping together among the girls was allowed as some were very homesick. There was not much harm in seeking warmth. She gathered in her insecurity, determined to become master of herself and not be intimidated by the girls. She would shoo them off into their own beds, whatever.

She heard movement. She flicked open the nearest curtain to see a neatly made bed unoccupied, altogether an eerie experience in the ghostly moonlight, and she shuddered. She flicked open the next curtain, and gasped. The passion of it was disgusting. There was no mistaking what Frances and Sophie were doing. Sheets and blankets had been thrown off by thrashing legs. Frances's thighs were clinging around Sophie's long, damp hair. The fair, page-boy cut of Frances's hair was bobbing up and down on top of Sophie's big belly not two feet from the postulant's eyes. The two girls evidently did not hear the rasping of the curtain rings or the nervous cough of the young woman in the grey serge outfit, who was paralysed by such close iniquity. She watched horrified for a few minutes, before she let out a scream and went running off past the windows and the cubicle curtains to wake a more senior nun.

Frances was always aware of the bravery of her action. She did not scuttle back to her own bed after the disturbance. Coldly conscious of the situation, she made the bed and placed herself in it beside Sophie, who had retrieved her nightgown and put its virginal white flannel all over her Venutian flesh.

Sophie was dismayed. She felt she was in a dilemma of two self-sacrifices and unable to choose. If she had been a selfish person, it would not have been hard to betray Frances. It was she who had influence in the school. Her dissemblances and excuses would have been accepted, and Frances would have been expelled.

The nuns would like a single, expellable scape-goat. But for the moment Sophie's brain was phased, and Frances seemed in control of herself. They embraced with a divided-we-fall-intensity, and Frances was ready. She was defiant and articulate.

The senior nun was flabbergasted, but not shaken to the core. It was the postulant who had seen it. Her inadequacy in the language necessary and the nun's limited imagination combined to give an inaccurate description of the crime. However, the Mistress of Discipline decided to make an example of them. Duly, she arrived in the dormitory and castigated loudly, intending to wake every sleeping-beauty-with-pimples within earshot.

The Reverend Mother, the following day, called a special assembly to shout 'hell-fire and brimstone' and to go red in the face about the ungodliness of lesbian practices. 'From now on,' she bellowed, 'no touching, no seeking warmth. This evil must not be seen in these buildings or within these grounds, it must not be allowed to cast its horrible degrading shadow in these halls again. It will not. Not during my administration. I will be no longer lax with this issue.'

The scandal shook the whole school, and went beyond. All parents, other public schools and a number of newsletters got wind of it. No expulsions, however, were carried out. While Frances's parents begged the Mother Superior to mend Fanny's dreadful ways with the severest punishments, Sophie's parents took it all in their stride. They were rich, tolerant, easy-going and happened to ease the Mother's concern with a gift of sporting equipment. The affair fizzled with the more far-reaching circumstances of exams, and end of term. Nevertheless, the scandal had scarred Frances.

Where Are You, Ellen Spalding?

The night brings you back into my mind, and I remember the word 'hate' embossed with the scabs of hairpin torture on both your arms. Your arms were a legend at the school, but your face has disappeared — disappeared among the crowds of girls who are dragged into custody for being 'exposed to moral danger'. Into those institutions I am afraid to even investigate as a sane conscientious journalist. I am afraid to see the colour of the paint on the walls, above and below the line at shoulder height. I envy your ability to spit and not be intimidated by them. I cry much more than you do for the punishment you get, for the bigness of the act and the smallness of your saliva. They tell me television is going into the Reformatory to make a serial. They will feed the living rooms hungry for sentimentality with happy endings. Spit, Ellen, spit, my girl. Let that saliva, no worse and no better than the Pope's, roll down the full gloss paint — catching the light. Cameramen pull out your focus, zoom in and make that little drip a drop of dew on a faded leaf; you dare!

Tonight is not the first time I've thought of Ellen Spalding. Of all the hundreds I've taught, of all the names I've ticked on a roll, I remember the name Ellen Spalding, but she was at the school maybe a month, maybe less — a disruption, of course. A class of the third year students — nubile girls, littler boys — in square desks along the long room. The rows disturbed by Ellen, a natural creator of chaos. And what did we have, that stern elderly nun and I, to control her with? She, her stick, her temper, her detentions; but against those you had your freedom, your fearless or imperative anarchy, your four-letter words, and you could deal as savage a hurt as she. A state of war with weapons. I don't suppose I wanted your love — that obsessive sado-masochistic infatuation with older women would have been too familiar to you. The round of orphanages providing you with a painful surfeit of aunties, you knew the cruel distance of their kindness. Many wounds, having no right to expect more. So what did I have, your young English teacher overwhelmed by the noise of third formers? 'Nothing!' reverberates and echoes in the deep chasm of your need, nothing. Not even the desire to enter the knotty web of your life, just respect for the pain and emotion of that word on your arms. Both. The guts of it, this product of an ungenerous society. Don't think for a moment, Ellen, that I was curious about you then. No questions were levelled by me as to your background to any more informed member in the gossip-warmed confidence of the staff room, not one. I overheard a little while I munched cold salty scones provided by a junior domestic science group. You see I was aware that society is a monster and people are its victims. You were my problem only forty minutes a school day; with the sigh and raised eyebrow of many a teacher I could suffer it through to the end. Ticking up a few more hours 'experience'.

When you ran away from the Home, and hence the school, you were talked about for a day, and then forgotten — information alone fuels interest. No one knew where you were... I had visions of you on the Hume lifting your thumb to passing trucks. Ellen on the road. Ellen cheeky and confident in her freedom. Ellen drinking the rain outside some roadhouse. Ellen ready to suffer and tackle anything. Through necessity. Necessity so absolute that it gave you jokes and philosophy. So I saw you popular, truckies and junkies providing you with a roof, food, piercing cans of beans with your eyetooth and obtaining all the skills of alley life. At first, I saw you riding FJ Holdens with skinheads through East Gippsland, inside the mysterious leopard-skin car seat privacy of that world. Your sneaky fears well covered with bravado. Once free, you were never a victim again. Not in my mind. The abuses to your person came under the heading of masochism and were your own. You remained superior. A woman with the indifference and infinite patience of mother earth. Plus the disinterest and cruelty to deal unplanned and sudden revenge — the secret to have nothing and be alone — ultimate distrust — pure righteous hate. Emblazoned on your forearms.

But you were only fourteen, and a fat unattractive girl, knocking about the classroom clumsily gathering bruises on your thighs and more for your store in insensitive insults, even from those whom you called your girlfriends. They, adventurous sophisticates from down the line, took you up as an oddity, as a source of stories and jargon on the volatile subjects, so fascinating and forbidden. That was obvious from the tone in the giggles you caused. Cats with a mouse. Their slight difference, Ellen, came from the fact that they or their parents were a cut above the average. Those brief friendships you had in that class were with the charmed, the lucky, and they delighted to use you. They delighted, also, after you left, in wearing expensive clothes, in following fashion . . . Do you know that one of them, the chief, actually is a model now? A slave to materialism, up to her neck in decadence and more of a whore than you could ever be, no matter how desperate your privation: believe me, Ellen. Yet I know with all your hate, you would feel more guilt than she. You have the dignity of woman, and feel the offences against mother earth. Indignity would make you angry. And it has nothing to do with how you seem on the streets in the eyes of the observers and keepers of the law. How you can laugh! How you can scream! How you can throw your insides to the wind from the top of the big dipper at Luna Park!

You think it's easy for me to write these things, Ellen, sitting in moderate comfort knowing that life will not knock on my door with rude demands. I have the luxury of a room and the choice of whom I wish to be with. I will not be disturbed, the mother nature in me will not be called to minister cures and comforts. There you are, still illiterate but bright and cunning, in the brown gloom of a flat behind the Cross, by-passing the joint as it goes round, waiting for the intrusion which will call upon your fundamental common sense. You would grow up, I think, to know people well, to understand and give advice — or perhaps your field is medicine. You know what to do for diarrhoea, hepititis, V.D. Can massage. Have a repertoire of herbal remedies.

It would gratify me as an old teacher to see you behind a microphone backed by a blues or rock band screaming out with full-lung passion, 'I'm an evil girl's daughter and you can't hurt me no matter what you do, oh no no no.' Insinuating a giggle through the power in your voice. And for what it's worth having fans trample each other to death for love of you. Mass love in place of the quiet oppressive security of Mum and Dad at breakfast time. That which you never had, and that which psychiatrists will say was all you really needed. 'Dear dear, the milk is spilt. All we can do now is find a mop and use it.' Any sort of a mop. With a certain type they could make you a model too, Ellen. Here is where I ask you to spit. With all the disgust of a have-not. Middle-class feminists will envy your parentlessness, having discovered the family is the root of sexist oppression. 'I'm an evil girl's daughter and I don't care what you say and do, oh no no no.' The real anarchy at the rear end of a corrupt society. 'I've been beat and I've been screwed, it don't make no difference to youse.'

I'm waiting to hear your name, Ellen Spalding.

It was a particularly bad day at school, for me. My engagement had just been broken. I did not have the emotional strength to direct the activity of thirty people for the next forty minutes. Especially as they would be enraged by the conduct of the stern elderly nun who preceded me in having the right to tell them what to do. Deaf to the rhythms of nature. Be late. Ruffle through the meagre teaching aids. A box of photographs. A cassette recorder. Laden with equipment, tools of distraction. 'Okay. Take a photograph. Listen to the music and write a poem. Respond to the audio-visual stimulus . . .' What? Erk. Oh. Do we have to? '*That* I had trouble getting. I'm trying to make your life more interesting. Just relax, go to town. Write whatever you like.' Do we get marks? Are you going to collect them? 'I don't know yet. Now get to work. I'll give you half an hour. Then I'll have a look. If they're good I'll mark them if they're bad I'll throw them in the rubbish tin.' Now to dream of my lost lover, and listen to the music. One photograph left and Ellen staring at me. Hate. Oh no. The picture left was by far the ugliest — a blank television set and a floating head of a baby. Repulsive. 'Ellen. Come here.' The walk expressed hate and reluctance, and I remember that I wished my life had not led me to cross the path of this girl. As she kicked the legs of others' desks and nudged their writing arms, I fantasised that I should take her outside, walk with my hand on her shoulder and ask her the meaning of the word on her forearms. If I could do that . . . she was beside me. Challenging. I silently picked up the ugly photograph and handed it to her, and motioned her back. The strength of indifference. Because I didn't care, the class was silent and the music played for thirty minutes. The machine clicked, snapping me out of daydream and the lethargy of melancholia. Besides, suddenly I was curious. 'Righto, either keep writing or read something else. I'll look at them now. If you talk I'll lose concentration. Then the only course of action will be to rip 'em up wholesale. And today's goody person can take them down to the incinerator and watch them burn.' You wouldn't dare. 'Wouldn't I?' Shshshs. They were pretty good and I lavished generous marks, rewarding them more for the half hour peace than literary quality. Ellen.

Yes, Ellen. I'll always remember your name. And that day. That repulsive photograph. The look of the page on which you had written: grade one lettering, quarter-inch high printing, uneven, abominable spelling . . . Yet my red pen was arrested mid-air as sharply as Abraham's dagger was above Isaac's body. I looked at you and you shrugged, distracted, wondering whether your girlfriends were about to make fun of you. I was embarrassed also. I couldn't whisper 'Beautiful!'

breathlessly as I now feel my response was. 'May I keep it?' You were surprised, almost generous, for a second. But 'Nup,' perversely. 'May I copy it out?' So I sat at your desk and copied it out reverently, speaking to you, poet to poet, suggesting where a line might end, a new stanza. You had no such finery, just words arranged like cows in a paddock. The baby challenges the television set with his life, his innocence, his ignorance. The television is dead. The baby will never contain as much knowledge, but the television set is dead. The blank affirmation of life. You, woman, with 'hate' engraved on your arms! 'Do you write other poems?' Of course not, never. What has happened to that spring of poetry, Ellen Spalding? An invisible dimension you had not indulged, do you indulge it now? Are you riding a Janis Joplin course from pimples to power, throwing yourself in with all your might, by now you would only be eighteen or nineteen? Or have you married already and weighed yourself down with babies and a man you control and who controls you, an ingrown toenail of a life? There are no middle of the road happy endings for you, my girl, not with that disastrous dichotomy. You ran away almost immediately after that day because I did not have another chance to educate the poetry in you, and I was disappointed. For with that affirmed, you would have had at least one staff to take with you on the road — but one little time? You did not believe me, might not have known that I knew. I could have convinced you had I time. But you were gone. The answers to my enquiries were horrifying searches and awful words like 'No they haven't picked her up yet.'

Please, Fate, I hope you turned that poetry into native cunning and warm womanliness so she escaped authority and was loved by her friends. Is.

Ellen, I believe in your inner freedom, I saw it. Where are you, Ellen Spalding?

Today I sat in a restaurant cupping a mug of coffee in both my hands, nodding.

'Yes, a poet can be illiterate.'

'How come she couldn't write?'

'Oh I don't know, pillar to post, school to school, punishment to punishment . . . '

'You don't believe in schools?'

'No way, that's an old argument of mine, don't get me on to it.'

'Whatever the particular art, it is a matter of environment, conditioning.'

'Yes if I could dance what I wrote I'd dance it.'

'Of course.'

'Art is the only thing that teaches. You know, you snap your fingers and say, "aha"?'

'Mmm?'

'I don't mean skills . . . '

'But you'd think if they were doing a series on the Reformatory and girls put away because they're exposed to moral danger, you'd think they'd tell the truth.'

'But the truth is hardest of all. It's so complex, the real understanding is not in knowing the facts.'

'But washing cars is hardly a happy ending. Yellow uniform. Actress smiles. Credits. Ads.'

'But it'd take a great writer, director, etc. to really convey. Or a great society.'

'Let's create Mighty Woman.'

'One way or another.'

How many people have kept you in bondage under the name of love, Ellen? Or are you still young enough to believe in the great miracle of happily-ever-after? But I imagine you have a serenity by now, an eighty-year-old eighteen-year-old . . . that you have become reliable in the disillusionment of it all . . . that your poetry has turned into useful philosophy, a pragmatic thing. Something as simple as 'You give and you get.' The sadness of that word on your forearms five years ago is that whatever life has done to you, it will not have given you, unless you have worked at obtaining the skills of an art, the means to translate its significance into something which will change society. I wish you hadn't written that poem, rather that I had taken you outside and forced you to tell me what hate meant — the poem was too easy. Distant. Maybe your real poem was your escape. Ellen on the road, fourteen, fat and courageous. Destined, according to sociologists, for the Wayside Chapel dependent on mainlining heroin. Mainlining heroin you may well be doing, wasting yourself, turning in on your hate — festering in a spiritual, social and physical sickness. I don't believe it, that gentle affirmation of life you gave me, and your sleeves were rolled to the elbows, was too deeply ingrained — at that young hopeful age you expected nothing. The tension between possibility and reality was set up ready. Friction. Fire.

Perhaps I superimpose my optimism on your life, which had it been mine may have plunged me into suicidal despair. Somehow I am here, remembering you and your name. My soft sensitivity over-reacting to the accidental and external; you have every right to scorn me in much the same spirit as you forbade me to keep your copy of your poem. I watched you passing the rubbish tins but I didn't see you screw it up, probably you did throw it away somewhere out of my sight. I would have kept that copy more carefully than the one in my handwriting, and I guess you knew that. Now you may scorn me for avoiding the social realities which have made your life a trial, social realities I am too weak to even observe and record — scorn me for wanting the sentimentality of fiction — scorn me for making you into a small heroine. Capable of scorn. Absolute.

Yet I'm crying for your shame, the babyish handwriting. Your hesitation in going up for that photograph. The pride of it! Don't let them touch that. Keep it wherever you are, Ellen Spalding.

The Rubbish Tin outside Federation Café

The hard lives are not mine, the young philosopher assumed, then thought. Stream of golden hair laughing falling, springs inside the soles of his feet; a walker, he walked, a charmed one. It is so clear that when he lies sideways on a couch there is a bowl of cherries near; and, should they be rotten, he would eat them with a smile. Good, very good world, he would say. He did not spend time with people, not a group nor a girl, nor a faithful friend. He had no partner-in-life, he was not *expected*. Nor was his calm aided by chemicals or smoke.

This is he who approached an octogenarian fossicking in the tin marked 'Litter Please' outside Federation Café

I am guilty of only my own punishment, he stopped disfocused mid-stride to complete or maybe to digest this sentence. Accidents are usually caused by stupidity. I am guilty of stupidity, I suffer the effects of an accident. I can be guiltless, learn guiltlessness, if I am not stupid, not punished. He was caught in a circle. He was motionless, unable to escape his sentence which seemed to pin his arms firmly to his sides. If I am guilty of laziness then laziness punishes me, he pursued. But there is the problem of what to do, what action to take . . . stock still in the street.

The octagenarian was a pianist, once. She was not looking for the remains of a meat pie to eat. She searched jerkily, jabbingly, for a twenty-cent piece which had slipped out of her arthritic fingers when she was removing the wrapping from her ice-cream. Nor was she enjoying that ice-cream which dripped and changed to stickiness in the crevices of her hands. Hence her anger.

But she has always been tone deaf. This is the knowledge of the unfortunate children who passed through St Peter's Church School between the years 1924 and 1959. Many remember the blood blisters, bruised knuckles and other embarrassments with a generous laugh: an indulgence of the days mercifully survived, proudly behind. Bob now manager of the local Post Office has neither forgiven her nor forgotten the tears he shed in front of the assembled school in 1954. In the past twenty years he has not sung; in fact in his bachelor flat is an unusually large collection of birds which have suffered the art of taxidermy; stuffed creatures of paradise in silent glass cages.

I have to believe I am right, certainty being the basis of belief, the young philosopher stated; his mind was blank, his legs were freed. He entered Federation Café and took a pint of milk with a straw. His fine blue eyes rested after a time on the woman at the tin. Rainbow jewels gathered in the white corners of the blue. A lump hindered his swallowing. For no reason the good earth and Malay peasants swinging buckets of rubber and singing occurred to him. Warmth released by this vision loosened his tight tears, which flowed. Over his nose through his moustache down the straw into the milk. Salt.

Rooming House

Time to change the fat, screaming out, and is it ever? Tender no comode-cleaning stomach of Trudy cavorting and somersaulting in her body walking through the hallway — wide tile tesselated floorway of a sandstone mansion in South Hobart, now flats and rooms to let with a shared bathroom, with a shared kitchen — grand wide stairway brown still in places otherwise whitened and hairy — halfway up a little stained glass window sparkling. Through all this weaves the misty pungent fume-form of black fat sizzling up spitting to cook fish. Fresh fish caught at the docks by the husband de facto who drinks in the pubs near the pier after fishing with cans of beer near — the evening meal is secure, dead blood scaly in a canvas bag. Mrs Slattery's eyes weep-red from flagons of sweet sherry as she emerges from rooms once servants' quarters and stumbles with her fish-in-newspaper at big empty square wooden table, swearing, as does the sizzling angry black fat, as the scaling sharp fish knife bruises white meat. She is swearing at him. Every night at six thirty she is swearing at him and the noise and the smell spill/flood out from the low-roofed narrow passage burrows behind the kitchen. Trudy's room is in the front, her window facing the big strong tree with a tyre-swing squeaking on it. There is a lilac near the sandstone fence. The rest of the garden is weed and dirt. Using the grand land of the old house to best advantage he has added prefab flats on the back. The rooms are cheap. Three or four other families are around, and bachelors and students, and a husband and wife entertainment team — seen better days, better venues . . . *You know that Carol 'Carnival' she'll never do any good, no sir, not a hope. I've been singin' in places around here for years, and before I came to Hobart . . . jazz singin' requires . . . bad expression you know, bad grammar . . . what's wrong with Carol apart from her voice bein' as*

thin as a sparrow's, is she sings everythin' too clearly . . . you gotta slur ya words and you never sing i-n-g 'ing', it's always 'in' . . . she clips her song, she reckons a song is words, well it ain't, it's sound, music . . . one continual sound . . . she hasn't got a heart in 'er mouth, she wouldn't have the soul to put out into the air . . . you get my meanin'? But it's no use me tellin' you, the good days've gone . . . she'll change 'er name a dozen times 'n sleep 'er way up, no one's got any ears any more . . .
Enormous Titian-haired woman lumbering housecoatedly and pretty pink floral prints all grubby deeper into the servants' quarters than the drunk's room; drummer husband and she have a pride and those who know the Hobart scene of honkytonk or good ol' jazz say they are the best but for the sax and clarinet, players of these come and go making the band uneven. They paint their faces, put on wigs, dress to the nines, walk important-swively-fussy, pursed-lip formality and familiar regularity to the pub on Saturday night to hear Winnie and Bill, Bill with his jokes, been going for years and Winnie with a voice to make you cry — with as many shandy or stout, they'll weep, they'll laugh, they'll shout, later maybe they'll fight, even on the street. Winnie and Bill, their darlings — with Rita, the brown-eyed red-haired child Shirley Temple cheeky until it's closing time; precocious spoilt little brat, say that to Winnie and see what happens.

A Book Is Launched In Soho

Confessions of a Butch Ballerina was the book. Every hustler and friend on the New York literary and media scene was at the party, the launching, though no copy of the book was in view. In fact there were no books in sight at all. Just people, alcohol, plastic cups and a ballet barre around the wall. Disco music came from somewhere and caught the ear of a few who continued to practise steps in front of the enormous mirror which covered the entire far end of the loft. The rhythmic were few, it seemed; or lovers. Most of the guests were stationary and upright, quizzing each other, discussing neuroses and generally working hard gathering copy. On the whole they were professional party-goers, adept at recognizing celebrities in a flash of the eyes. However, no one could distinguish or point out with absolute certainty the authoress.

For a while the general attention was focused on a feminist. She had a bad back and was wearing a loudly printed kaftan, and from a distance, appeared to be answering questions with an informed togethering of the eyebrows, and was obviously conscientiously mixing. One of the in-group of gossip-hustlers soon learnt that she was in fact a City politician deeply concerned with the development of the South Bronx and had made the papers by publicly disagreeing with the Mayor on this issue. Everybody there was 'important', and she not least, for the rise of the hard-headed woman is one of the hopes of American politics. These were the women who had overcome the need for sex and/or husbands, who had learnt through so many Ingrid Bergman and Katherine Hepburn movies that the strong woman cannot happily have children and career so they'd willingly foregone children to devote their lives to the general freshening-up of the American Way. By publicly supporting abortion reform they diminished their own mystery to some extent, but remained stoutly silent on the question of homosexuality.

So she was not she. The authoress was not there. Her absence was, anyway, only of secondary interest to the majority of the gathering for always their first concern was themselves. *The Culture of Narcissism* got discussed by these cultural narcissists, and was quickly judged to be a slick cultish book. Christopher Lasch, needless to say, was not present. The room comprised equally males and females, a small minority of whom had arrived in couples. In perhaps the largest group was the middle-class Jewish woman, single-divorced-or-separated, inside whose skull the following stream of thought flowed: 'I will say I'm reactionary. I will. For I do want a deep meaningful relationship with a man and children. The modern day liberalism is not fair. I will thrust my neck out and discuss Freedom from the opposing point of view. I just want a man. I must finish my paper. What time is it? Where's my pocket book? Is it firmly locked? I'm for the return of ethics and morality in psychoanalysis. I mustn't eat. I mustn't smoke. These are bad for me. The more wine I drink the more likely I am to take someone home with me. Too much and I will cry for the things in the world I have not got. I will keep myself in order, and be home by 11.30 and get down to work with my books. No one must know my age.' She studied the crowd for those who looked particularly intelligent and interesting, preferably of the masculine gender between the ages of 35 and 45 and of medium build and respectable height. She never went anywhere with less than fifty dollars in her purse and rarely spent more than five dollars. It was a matter of principle; thus one could be generous if a surprise situation called for it.

She sought out her friend, an author. He, a large man, was fascinated by the amazing fact that this woman earned a considerably large sum by listening to 'patients' on the telephone for forty-five minutes and, though reasonably attractive, she did not attract. His hunger for copy was dumbfounded minute by minute by her incredible ignorance of human nature and the world. He wondered whether she were truly mad or was this normal? In the interests of his work he kept the answer to this question up in the air. In the air between his nose and the mouth of his inquisitor, the state of Western civilisation was being examined in its supreme capital, New York City, at the parties of Downtown Manhattan's Intelligentsia! 'Bohemian' was a word he would soon use with a new slant.

The authoress at the time of the party was hating herself for what she had done. Fortunately, in New York, it was snowing: fresh thick white flakes blunted the edge of the wind that drove it down at an angle of about 60°. Just seeing it cover 2nd Ave was a delight which settled gently on top of her emotional and moral misery, 'chilling the subways of her heart'. It was for phrases like this that she'd written her book in the first place; they wouldn't leave her alone. Phrases like the title, for instance.

The truth was the title of the book put off most people assembled to celebrate its coming. It hadn't been a difficult operation: half an hour on the telephone leaving explicit messages on either recorded or live answering services telling who else was to be there; hiring a Creative Movement teacher's loft in the right area in Soho; and the firm belief that such an operation was absolutely necessary for the book to be a real book. Multiple covers were pinned to the inside walls of the 'john'; these portrayed a silhouette of a dancer reflected in a mirror, light catching the edges of an afro cut making it appear fair, and behind the booklike angle of the mirror the background was Marlboro red. Thus some conversation of its existence was occasioned by those people returning from relief of the bowels or bladder not absolutely obsessed with their own descriptions and definitions. Some, not much.

The prominent reviewer's insides were in a knot as she sat there. It was something she hadn't even told her analyst, how meeting a particular type of man in a particularly common situation tied the muscles at the base of her bladder together as securely as if the urine inside were a dreadfully dangerous substance which upon no account should be allowed out into the air. This evil was exacerbated by her awareness that its volume increased at an alarming rate. The awfully basic frustration had brought her to tears as she stared unseeingly at the red black and white cover of the book she ought to be noticing. The clamour of people at the door was the clamour of the SS in the middle of the night. 'Stupid dark blood memories,' she murmured, and the six small posters came into focus. 'Good God what could it possibly be about?' she asked her brain; with this the piss trickled gratefully into the water closet, slowly, with reluctance, so she continued to concentrate almightily on the title and the sexy photograph of a dancer. It was after having had an extremely private experience that she emerged, elbowing her way confidently through the throng of party-goers who joked while she laughed at how long she'd been inside; they like people in the supermarket line with only one purchase, would have been far quicker. She smiled bitterly, with brilliance.

'. . . In my book, dance is an image . . . I don't know . . . for everything in me that's black and dark and free.' She was slurring her words, 'For a kid, dance and play's the same — ever thought that? Only people under the age of ten can enjoy freedom.' Cause they don't discriminate nothing from nothing . . . but it happens earlier, real early.' She leaned in comfortable drunkenness, both elbows on the bar. 'Dance is really a sophisticated, grown-up game, that is ballet you know, but it has come under the kill-joy hands of the archbishops of power. They divided the kingdom and what do you have? the warring states — dance, sex and religion and everybody's confused.' There were enough *simpatico* places for her to be making her way slowly downtown to the address scribbled on a matchbook in her pocket, and seem not to be, and seem to

intimacy. These flash girls like eagles will descend and devour the tenderest ailing prey with the pathetic glint of weakness in its eye. They were, on the whole, far too intelligent and worldly to be able to put up with the aggressive brutes of old. Rednecks from the South and bores from the Midwest were out. No matter where they themselves originated, these New York career girls soon developed a nose for a manageable neurosis — conversation grist psychosis — in the men they desired. How disappointed, contemptuous and superior they were when they discovered after a one-night stand with the man of their dreams that they had frightened him into disappearance. For not to be beaten in anything they all have a healthy rapacious sexual appetite. Statistics being what they are, a goodly number of their one-night stands turned out to be nonserious affairs with bores from the South and rednecks from the Midwest. Thus they had a taste of their own pathos, a sensibility they might share with the right man when he comes along, finally, eventually, and free. Meanwhile, they have the excellent backstop of a successfully and financially rewarding career. So it was among her own that the reviewer found herself when she entered in her fur coat. Woody Allen did arrive about half an hour later in the company of friends. He recognised no one except the bartender and appeared to be in a bad humour.

In the loft where a teacher taught Creative Movement the author had stayed longer than he'd meant. In New York City the men are the gossips. They exchanged knowing glances over the headtops of the women who were interested in more serious matters. The psychologist in particular wore an extremely serious expression behind the curtains of her hair. The author was tempted to finger these curtains away, but the gesture would have been read to mean a sexual come-on and he was determined to return to his home-loving lady and their enlightened relationship. But for the moment he was exasperated for she was stubbornly refusing to reveal to him details of the sickness or even the anonymous troubles of her telephone patients and what she said and did to cure them.

Her private Hippocratic oath was making him behave as if he desired her companionship in bed for the night, and this was the reason for her intensely serious countenance, not as he figured the ethical struggle to tell or not to tell the things he most desperately required to know, his profession being his and hers hers. No, she was imagining his home-loving lady whose name and nothing else she knew and, patently, she could not give him this night because there was no future in it, even though this was about the fortieth party he had told her answering service about. She was struggling with the concepts of 'friend' and 'lover', neither of which she knew the real essence. There were, however, many words in the air between his nose and her mouth. Her eyes lifted no higher than the pocket of his coat.

Although she was not, as the social workers at Bellvue had written in the report, troubled by a passive-aggressive personality and childhood schizophrenia, the authoress did find the clash between herself and the realities of life at times difficult to bear. The books she spent her time with were the classics, her heroes thus men and her ambition to have a patriarchal wisdom similar to that of such venerable elders as Socrates and Thomas Moore. She loved women who were feminine and to whom she could play the courtly Astrophel, honour, bestow favours upon and protect. She had a rigorous humanistic philosophy and believed in a god who resembled Plato's Form of the Good. Therefore she was forever comforted from the inside by a private elitism, and books in the public libraries are many that feed this spring, albeit anachronistic and in unbelievable contrast to the fit, black bejeaned body that housed it.

The *Confessions* were full of lightness-darkness symbolism; inside was as bright as the White Tornado Knight and outside the world was as dark as the cellar that confined her some of the years of her childhood. Yet she was lucky and optimistic and full of tolerant encouragement for her sisters who were battling oppression in the political sphere.

Of experimental writing, now. Form cracks open and contents spill out, as sticky, fascinating and loose as the yolk of an egg. Mess. Messy. People who judge too soon reach for a mop. Whatever is there goes into the rubbish bin. They try to flush it down the sink.

Dismiss it. How many reviews do this! They dismiss without examination or twist the new writing into some preconceived notion of their own. How many editors' readers do this! Tell the writer how it should have been done! Reach into the back pockets of their own heads for formulas. 'The form goes around the content, see, and there you have an acceptable shape. A workable bit of literature. Packaged. Clean. Fits in the cupboard. We could sell it like that. Only like that.'

It's as if the actual meaning of words has been forgotten and replaced with something else. 'But I am a creative writer. Every fibre in my being aches to be original. I live on the edge of what has been done.' You turn around once, twice, scratch the head. They're saying it's elevating form over content. It's formalist.

What about the mess of broken sentences, thoughts coming in from everywhere, the rhythms of abrupt, here it is? Behind your back they've cleaned it away and are examining the broken shell. They're handling the bits of egg-shell with delicacy as if they're afraid of hurting your precious ego. The original is unseeable. You've been had again by the old Confidence Trick — the trick of confidence.

You can only turn about and go away, and as you walk or drive or sit on the tram, train, plane or bus or swing a bit on the playgrounds in the park, you think.

One thinks and thinks. How impossible is the judgement of the judges! What do they know! The jargon of the shells! And, you know, someone will come along, someone with a confidence trick of her own. In a box with cotton wool is a collection of broken egg-shells. This author is really careful about presentation, she handles the box as if the very cardboard and cotton wool could break at the merest bump and she presents the judges with this creation, trumpeting her creativity and artistic nature.

Who Cares About The Sentence?

When I first visited Kris Hemensley with the purpose of talking about writing, I said the role of the sentence had changed. It was the first time that the thought had occurred to me. In the nineteenth century writers of both factual and fictional prose felt that a whole thought is expressed and completed within one sentence. The next sentence would express the next whole thought in the logical order of their arguments of descriptions. There was delight in the very roundness of this discipline. The author was all powerful — it was an autocratic and imperialistic way of writing. The men and women of the nineteenth century felt in control of the forces created by man whether they be things or theories. Men and women of the post Second World War period feel far from in control of those horrific forces. My contention has no authority, however I hang on to the rudiments of my idea and present them as no more than that.

The role of the sentence has changed. Indeed the sentence in contemporary work can survive without making *sense* in itself and often without tense. One word, any word, can be posed between two full stops and although it is not an exclamation we will accept it. We will understand it. We will not accuse the author of laziness or obscurity. Yes she has broken rules, not our rules, but rules which preclude the author having control of the knowledge she is dealing with. The contemporary vocabulary is wide and although we hear and even use some words of whose origin or component definition we have not complete understanding, such words filter from the jargons of specialised fields into common usage. We have common usage understanding of them. That, of course, is a relative scale — common usage being at one end of the axis and specialised definition at the other: your position on the axis depending on the depth of your knowledge of the specialised field. It is stupid to suppose one has knowledge of all specialised fields, but I contend we do have awareness of them. More awareness than nineteenth century writers who are governor of their own territory and rarely step beyond it. Such questions as — why aren't readers of Jane Austen aware that one of the greatest military defeats in history is happening while Mrs Bennet is taking tea with Mr Collins? — are not asked. She wouldn't have dared. (There are many ways of putting this and none of them are safe from justified contradiction.)

The things which have happened to the political and intellectual world have had their effects on the techniques of writing. Compulsory or democratic education, popularisation of specific fields of learning, mass communication and the proliferation of audio-visual means of entertainment to mention too few. The result (a small part thereof) is that writers and their audiences have much inarticulated and inarticulable knowledge in their heads. Another result is that the creative writer, though she may have a territory, is not governor. Psychologists, sociologists, environmentalists and so on and so on, not to mention the bricklayer who reads the paper and watches TV, have some knowledge of the motivations, despairs, what-have-you, in the world of the writer.

What I'm saying is that now a sentence can be used as a hint rather than the means to express the whole thought. At times it is either not necessary or impossible to express the whole thought. (I don't speak of all sentences or of all thoughts.) Too much echoes in the mind of the reader for the writer to waste time on a technique whose roots are in explanation, where no explanation is needed. Or the writer may choose to use the inexplicable or the inarticulable thought or image; i.e. a noun which doesn't *do* anything or a verb which has no subject . . . etc.

A word has many possibilities — it is like a colour on a stage set, in effect at the mercy of the colour of the light shone upon it. The creative user of words knows about the magic of light — that her purple word can become green in a chosen context. The factual writer — (that is one way of implying the difference between a novelist and a historian, a short story writer and a sociologist, a poet and a philosopher) — must, because her purpose is explanation requiring accuracy/precision, the light shone on her words is straight daylight or white, least-imaginative electric light. The creator wants the viewer to have shocks and reverberations in her own private frame of reference, wants her imagination to take flight, wants to give her more than is written. For accuracy and precision, the explainer must endeavour to cut out the shocks and reverberations, must try to prevent her words journeying into the unknown parts of the reader's imagination. One of the ways of forcing the reader to take the word with exact, indisputable meaning is putting it into the *complete sentence*. Making it an object of a certain verb, or a verb of a certain noun, etc. Language as sign-writers' paint as opposed to language as artists' paint.

The language of the nineteenth century writers — too broad and beautiful to be treated in a flippant and simplified way — relied to a large extent on the formalism of the sentence. Not because they were preventing it journeying on its own to the reader's meaning, but because the writers were, in a way, explaining their imaginative vision. The public, just learning the joys of a monthly press and the lessening of illiteracy, did not have the fund of knowledge our public has. It was not bored by the written word — written fiction did not have the tremendous rivalry it has today. In giving our vision we must rise above, beyond, out of the need to explain that which is known and which is being known explained would bore the reader and bog down the writer. So it has come in some cases that the vision is the vision of language, the creation the creation of language (not bound by formal constructions), the language the language of contemporary confusion, broad knowledge, much inarticulation, a game of words and information. The rhythm of contemporary life is not the rhythm of the rounded complete sentence.

Nun

The pregnant nun. The aborted nun. The frigid nun. The frustrated nun. The contented nun. The silent nun. The saintly nun. The mean nun. The proficient nun. The greedy nun. The secretive nun. The conservative nun. The radical nun. The inspired nun. The desired nun. The nun and the gardener. The nun and the priest. The nun and the monk. The nun and the altar boy. The nun and the pupil. The nun and the parents. The nun and the strap. The nun and the vegetables. The nun and the nun. The nun and the plane ticket. The nun and the university. The nun and the mother. The nun and Mother Ireland. Nun in a habit. Nun in a skirt and court shoes. Nun in a slacksuit. Nun on an expedition. Nun at a seminar. Nun in the suburbs. Nun in the city. Nun in the country. Nun in a taxi. Nun at the driver's side. Nun with glasses. Nun and kitten. Nun suffering the little children. Nun at the organ. Nun on a record cover. Nun with a bottle of brandy. Nun smoking a cigar. Nun on horseback. Nun on a tram. Nun in a pub. Smiling nun. Weeping nun. Melancholic nun. Jolly nun. Frozen nun. Sweaty nun. Nuns in the sea. Nuns around a bathing box. Nun in a sauna. Blushing nun. Bruised nun. Nun feeding the goldfish. Nun counting out the money. Nun throws herself off high-rise. Nun buries herself. Nun rises. Nun without a vocation. Nun on the road to heaven. Nun with an anklet of thorns. Nun with a diamond ring. Nun in the dark. Nun photographed. Nun without relatives. Freelance nun. Poor, chaste, obedient nun. And, finally, nun with a toothache.

Happening Upon A Character, In The First Person

When I look up from a prone naked position, when I lift my eyes into Bedlam, and call myself (her) Hystia in that nick of time caught (say) between the blank and the completed form. For the moment a paperless identity: and not a fully-fledged marked and marketed product, a named and numbered person. When, to be brief, I create myself again so that I (she) might walk and talk and partake in that hostile shoulder-rubbing jostle we tend to excuse on the basis that we are gregarious animals and civilised to boot and need to live where civility is enforced by law, in 'armed' civilisation riddled with technology and manufacture and economy and religion, when I am forced (I force her) to confront the confusion which swarms like an organisation of flying ants biting and intruding on her person, I am (she is, of course) overwhelmed by a feeling of depression.

Though not hysterical; irritated and incompetent, stumped and stumbling, never-at-a-loss-what-to-do, Hystia is willing to sit anywhere and dream. Let her eyes gloss over and locate themselves in another place, no need of drugs but alcohol, nicotine, antibiotics, herbal tinctures, vitamin supplements, analgesics, barbiturates, carbohydrates, carbon monoxide, caffeine, tannin and refined sugars, she is, now, hurrying to be alone in the sun with no clothes and nothing to attend to. (I remain in my prone naked position lifting up my eyes.)

It goes without saying that it is a huge step forward — a leap! — for her to expose her real carnal self to the gross expanse of windowed wall towering three storeys above (my) two square metres of straw. Behind the windows live all manner of bitter and twisted flat-dwellers, one or two of whom have purchased a cheap pair of binoculars for the sole purpose of searching

Hystia's pubic hair for evidence of crabs or lice, thus reaching some sort of conclusion about her sexual habits. Perhaps they have seen (me) itch. Hystia does not dissolve into full frontal self-excitation; I would not condemn her free dreamsome thought to boredom of the mind. There are other times for that. Probably a watcher behind the sky-reflecting glass is a mean man, a timid lad, a gentleman out of work, who spends his time inside until about five p.m. when he ventures (in his shiny brown, tapered, above ankle trousers) down to the pub. His hands are thrust deep into the pockets of his never well-shaped cardigan, and the lines on his face spell *unprivileged* and the shape of his mouth states emphatically: 'not a recipient'. Hystia does not anticipate harm at the hands of this man *in the present conditions*. His consent to the violence perpetrated against women is assumed, but no more energetic than the wobbling of the vocal cords. His large wife has a sense of humour and teenage sons who happen to be her allies. These sons have already been to the tatooist and had injected on their freckles indelible loyalty to 'MUM'. But Hystia is thinking not of rape this moment: it occurs to her that the totally privileged are sharks which have never been wounded, have never seen their own blood, can be polite and their niceness costs them nothing; the ones to fear are the partially privileged who even losing a little of their own blood are after someone else's; and the unprivileged are generous and know its cost. The swarm of flying ants. (I scrutinise the empty air so well I can see every particle of light.) Hystia might think as she carelessly notices that the flight of flies is sharply angular, possibly within a circle they do not describe the circumference . . . do not describe, she thinks: we have to be careful because we are afraid, we are afraid because we are careful, we are not totally paranoid because we are sufficiently careful, if we are not sufficiently careful we will succumb to a condition known as certifiable paranoia, and if we are certifiably paranoid, we forsake the circumference of normality and become a tangent; we are careful not to become a tangent because we are afraid of becoming a tangent because we do not know any more what we are afraid of, except perhaps we are afraid of being purely and simply afraid and we no longer know exactly what to be afraid of.

(Plot.) It is about five p.m. when too many shadows stretch across Hystia's fine brown flesh and goose pimples spread from her armpits down the insides of her upper arm. She yawns and flexes all the muscles of her limbs and closes her eyes for a moment before moving. Having done nothing, nothing at all, she feels free. Free now to do. (I find I have burnt the toast and boiled the kettle dry, and remark to myself, as friend once said, Doris Lessing worked through the problem of getting her characters from the supermarket into the car and home. I grinned, have grinned, do grin, will grin again.)

That one must pay for one's eccentricities even Hystia dismissed as a solution to her present problems. The phrase slipped out months ago — of her mouth as it pursued a rather sharp-edged tack in an argument she chose to call a discussion — and she had remembered it after, during one of those urgent times she reserved for Thought — her 'doing nothing' — to construct a backup logic. In any discussion she could defend it: one must pay for one's eccentricities.

The things she chose to do, she discovered, although she was convinced of the sanity of her desire to do them, were to be considered henceforth 'eccentricities'. This is not to say that most people did not do them at one time or other in their lifetimes — it was just that the social centre of behaviour remained anachronistic and people's minds often followed their lips and served the core — thus to be awake all night, smoking cigarettes end to end, swigging the remains of whisky and green ginger wine and downing litres of powdered coffee and hot water in pursuit of a particularly tantalising idea which struck with rude impatience at a truly inopportune instant, is not really unusual. Yet, even as dawn coldly whitened the world, this tantalising idea did not reveal itself to be of real substance (but flirtatious it was like a sprite sent thither to induce a person to self-destruct slowly . . . and with a human, full responsibility!).

The following day, her nerves nestled on razors, her stomach seized, her throat could hardly swallow and, to top it all, her mental processes congealed around the wound delivered by an unrealised possible truth — congealed into a dense list of unrelated, trivial insights. This eccentricity was (secretly) her 'work'. The problem was one of sanity.

(Coming to terms with oppression.) She was tempted to think that right now she should be indulged. It is not easy to articulate to others when the legs of the mind feel as if they are suspended over a bottomless pit. It is not easy to make oneself clear. But suicide, Wilde said, is the highest compliment one can pay to society. Her ovaries ached. The doctor treated her for hypochondria. On the way on the tram from the surgery she felt she was on the verge of hysteria (the exact moment for thought [thought so charged it is the realisation of experience] memory, observation, a logic too mathematical to be questioned) and through the tears resting on her wild eyes she saw misery greater than hers. The others there were not as free. And Sartre said you can know nothing without suffering for it? You can suffer without knowing, without blame: ignorance is no excuse for anything. The odd cruelty of learning drizzled into the seized machine of her spirit. (The reluctance of one plagued with despair!) It was in the park — the tram at this moment rattling beyond the next stop — a foreign man chose to step from behind a tree with his erect penis protruding from the two sides of his zip. She was offended by this assault and, simultaneously, aware of her own superiority. She did not say anything, and her strength and power would have been no different if he had thrown her on the ground and raped her — the extent of the pain was but relative. He did not. She was assaulted by the ignorance and violence that produces such acts in the city's parks: she was assaulted in the grain of her mind: and knew at once this performance was the same as being bashed over the head with knuckledusters, her own sexuality had nothing to do with that exposed genital organ: it was the dickhead of a violent oppressive society. A society which chose to know nothing about life, sex and freedom. Hysteria at this point might have been a release, but no, she was cold with total awareness, and the fear was just a reality.

She walked away no longer paranoid. Illusion had been cut away and lay like the bloody rags on the floor of the medical tent in war that had clung to a limb which might have been amputated. She felt enormously intact, almost jolly, as if a spent mental emotional and physical condition was where she must be right now. Her ovaries ached, but the pain was her own (own). Her chest ached but the cigarettes smoked the night before were her own choice (choice, the pursuit). Her sexuality was bruised by visual assault, but this was herself, a woman, everywoman, refusing to be blind. The man was pitiable, and ironically her genuine like of humanity began reviving itself; she cared.

I think it is possible to believe there is nothing to live for. (I've never written that before.) In the maze all avenues close off, suddenly. And the search is depressing. The maze is the self. Unknown live parts of the self set up trip wires when the way seems clear. The particulars are boring. I have no knowledge any more. We sit around like Aboriginals with our booze, some core thing stolen, and we've forgotten when it happened. We recall the recent past, powerlessness.

A Bit Of The Learning Bit

There was nothing ever to say about poetry in Eng. Lit., nothing ever. Something is wrong. Here we are in the classroom, a long way from a feeling Mae felt she remembered when she first read one of the poems. Which she could not recall in the spaces between the crisscrosses of her distractions — it was nothing much anyway, a bit of a warmth like suddenly finding oneself in a slant of sunshine soon to be obliterated by a cloud or the inexorable turning world. A heliocentric moment, the big world slotting itself into inevitable concentric spheres, a harmony which cannot always be experienced — her emotions were involved. It did not seem fair to the poet either — she raised her hand to say (at this point in her life she could not control her spoken word) — how could it be fair to anyone, she said, not to read everything they wrote? The class laughed. The nun coloured. Mae wanted to weave her way aloud through the tangle of words and responses in her mind — a poem's but a little window, one glance from a person, how do you know what it means all by itself? What do you attach it to? It's . . . she was interrupted. She now blushed deeply for whatever was being said on behalf of authority she took to be sarcasm. She seemed fated to be outside the conspiracy that enveloped everybody else. The poem now was a dead objective thing lying on her desk, a little pattern of rhymes and rhythms and words that seemed horribly formal and related to times past where lots of things were different — a piece of Sanskrit. To save herself and what she remembered of a feeling (she now remembered that there was a feeling), she began to concentrate on the nape of another girl's neck. Examine it for its beauty, use the magnetism of her look to make her turn around so that she might again receive pleasure from the profile — she let her sentimentality run riot. In this way she destroyed a capacity to memorise formulae, to keep in her head things which weren't what she called attached to her soul. It was, of course, the soul that mattered. Poems, she hoped, were products of the soul.

But Janice was making her soul ache. Knowing Janice had taken all freedom from her mind — Janice and she had once (once) embraced in a shower room, and from that day six or seven months ago, she had not been free from obsession. It was as though a demon of failure had overtaken her — some frustrated witch from olden times inhabited her and was pursuing a purpose her host, Mae Rose Murphy, did not understand and yet had to puzzle and cope with -- and Janice, from that moment in the shower room, had joined forces with the enemy and withdrew her favour and sympathy. Mostly superior but often threatened and frightened she avoided any close or one-to-one contact with Mae. Perhaps she was not mean.

The profile did come into view and it glared disapproval at Mae who replied to it with a goonish grin — melting, pleading, cowering and wagging her tail like a puppy. Scorned. The bell rang and the years clicked out with mechanical monotony and it seemed she would never find escape from that same abject servility.

Spit on the different one. Or make a giant your slave today.

Learning then confounded on the rocks of her emotionality, and sank. She became worshipping and had thus in enquiry to make her lovers her teachers. (Poems written in the sand cannot embarrass you so much. 'You always were a dreamy little thing,' her first woman said years later when Mae confessed to becoming a writer. It is no matter, just one of the small things one loves to remember. 'I always was a dreamy little thing, I have it on the best authority.')

Something must be done about this distraction — this Zorro-slash of heroism and mortification — this lack of concentration, this thing the moment it encounters something engagingly educative it wants to race away with renewed energy on to something else, no matter what: a person, place or book: a thing too impatient, it always finds itself arrested in nothing and looking back, both too late and too early. This fragmentation. This probable avoidance of the union of imagination and logical thought which could be the groundwork of freedom. (Daydreaming *par excellence* does not justify your being a writer, Maeve . . . the winter beach witch cackles invisibly while the wave comes up to take the poem away.)

Novel In Ten Lines

Leone's room is not near the left bank of the river where she drowned. Harold walked by the park bench, thinking. Thoughts of how and when and guilt were his and we are interested, also, in the clothes he wears, the trench coat with *Giovanni's Room* by James Baldwin in the pocket. Leone came from the country with blond hair that turned dark in the city — her cotton print dresses turned to brown pleated skirts. Leone was lonely. And Harold felt sorry, that's all. He had other friends, and lots of nights with other men: his own problems.

The Illusive Quality Stories

First

The roses are not real. Fading crêpe-paper roses rest neatly on the props table, lights will give them dewdrops, fingers will give them meaning, each night they have a moment of life. But they are crêpe-paper — outside it rains as I stare down at them.

Theatre is dangerous for me, I fall in love. I become, in fact, the inarticulate, blubber-mouthed, blushing lovelorn character of many plays, the comic character who is so extravagant he couldn't possibly take himself seriously, and who therefore will slope off alone, cruelly discarded, yet unscathed. The essence of these characters is that they lack courage, and for all their passionate yearnings they lack passion: they are always afraid of love. The poet as coward. Vampire. Parasite. Subjective reflector. Movie screen on which life plays and repeats its domestic comedy. Unsmiling protector of humour. Person who writes down such things as, 'A sense of humour is actually the innate knowledge that all things will pass', after much walking with drooped head, much sitting in an armchair staring into an open fire, after much, for want of a better word when a person appears to be doing nothing else, thought. Indeed he is a brilliant audience.

Never invite a brilliant audience backstage. Nor should he ever be involved in the theatrical process, for he will insist on helping with the wardrobe, then will not only break all the needles on the machines but sew up finger holes in gloves and accidentally cut through the centre of expensive cloth; or he will offer to do the carpentry, in which case the sets and raised areas will rock and be dangerously insecure until new wood is bought and all is remade. Harmlessly sitting in on rehearsals, he will clap or laugh helplessly at the mistakes, grow misty-eyed over the casual affection actors show each other and fall jealously in love with the imaginary creature of actor-character combined, doomed, fortunately, to a tragically brief existence. On first night, he will find the production the sum total of all that was boring, dull and stereotyped during rehearsals, but so deep will be his excitement at having at last a say that he will speak his perceptive, well-worded, disastrous criticism so loudly that the critic from a tabloid newspaper will gratefully overhear and damn the play in the morning press.

My words light and disappear, as I watch; drops of water?

The poet-coward is never entirely duped by the fantasy of theatre, he is above all a realist, he lives in the world outside. The world outside is to him, theatre. This character is dangerous. He has a loose tongue, he does not know what is important, he does not believe in love! He will play the clown, the fool, the baby to attract your secrets, and then they are public because people listen to the poet-coward. They seek his company, they know his power, they see the pen on his desk and nod with respect. They even come to him for clairvoyance. And nor will you know his sex. If he seems male, it it likely he's a eunuch. If she seems female she may be a hermaphrodite. The monster walks in the garden of our souls, for we all love a poet-parasite. He lives off the red love in the veins of other people, many people per single poet-vampire; without love he would languish and die. Although it is not true of everybody, it is true of the poet-parasite that the world owes him a living — he lives constantly in its debt, his forehead twists into a frown of guilt and responsibility; the troubled thinker!

Be gay my troubled thinker, and dance — the music has you jigging (you skipped as a child on the way to school making fairytales to your own fancy, lunging at shrubs, the swordsman of Monte Cristo) — the dance is but a skip, your hands are held, you swing around, reminded of peasants and dreamers, swept into a past. Your hands become damp. You blush. Pantomimes (the house lights went down, you clasped the cellophane of sweets so fast your palms sweated, you held your breath. The aunt beside you, doing her holiday duty, shuffled in her bag for the handkerchief she needed. You blotted her out. Waited, watched for the machinery to work, you missed that for the sudden delight of colour and costume . . .). The music stops.

I stare up into the roof of the rehearsal room searching for words which will transmit the steel crossbeams, the leads and the high-powered encased lights to another reality, trying to keep the casual humour of function. Turn the lights away from the sun, blacken the windows, let's have the paper roses lit with dew so that I am no more than a heart, loving. Give me a spot, a sphere, diameter my height, of love to accompany me as I walk away, into the street — she waves to me, a mere acquaintance. An individual's life seems so small, a handful.

I follow her, yes, I follow her. She drives the family's second car, an Austin A40 about '53, leaning forward peering over the wheel, and brakes suddenly. Scents of the character she plays drift back, ghosts of forgotten hugs. We are creeping along a tree-lined suburban street; which house is hers? The poorest, tricycles on the longish grass, a small wire-covered fishpond, white weatherboard; the Austin A40 crawls up the two strips of concrete and stops at the side of the house. I do not stop; she has not recognised my car. (The television room was also a sewing room, the children ignored their mother, feet on schoolbags watching.)

Nothing is easy for me. Every instant is fractured with words — words are like cracks in the concrete block of now. I stand five foot four and I say, 'I am in love. I love so many people and I am loved by many people.' The moment is made of emotion and yet I am outside it, drawing lines across the surface, words. Falsities. She stares, playing a quizzical smile, a smile of cunning questioning silence, hiding. In response to her cunning, I open up, speaking too many words, waiting for the wedge and the hammer blow. I can crumble. I can crumble. But I continue to talk arrogantly of love, for if the wind should change, if I should suddenly cease, I would have love on my lips. It is too much, she does not know what I expect of her; she punctuates her silence with, 'Well!' I understand her distaste. She sniffs an insincerity, she smells a selfishness and an absence of herself — she holds the unwanted gift loosely, her movements so deliberately slow. (Yes my love was the revival of dormant emotions. I walked into the television room, she was sewing. I tripped on my schoolbag, felt her smile. I had lied, and would not plead into her eyes, blushing. She stopped the machine, got up, came to me, lifted my heavy chin, grabbed my eyes with her own and hugged me.)

The actress captures . . .

The poet-coward does not want his love of the imaginary creature of actor-character combined to become a burden for the person of the actor. Certainly his love has wild hopes for happiness, plans for the future, traps and dreams, but this hope is not accompanied by the belief that dreams come true. No, dreams have enough truth in themselves to satisfy him. His dreams are written on concrete walls all over town; he is a realist, he realises the reality of dreams. There are certain buildings about the city that he frequents, dens and temples to the Dream, 'theatres'. The poet-hero carries a pantomime in his heart down dark alleys, over rainwet flagstones, on to scenes of muggings and bashings, faces brick walls examining patterns for hours, careless of malevolent knives, innocently alone. Why is this fearless one destroyed by a frown of disapproval?

I hurry away hurt, the world does not love me, again I have confused daydream with actuality . . . my heart won't learn.

The actress takes pity, she is not an imaginary creature. She is herself, a mystery to me. She peers over the steering wheel and the windscreen wipers brush at the raindrops on the glass.

Second

The roses she has torn off a wild creeper draw blood from her fingers. Proud of white plastic shoes as of a poverty, she steps deliberately, gingerly, through the mud; I stride beside her — this Australian heath is familiar to me — the track leads up the hill, dusk is grey-blue and olive green. The rain. Both Celtic heads of hair curl upwards. Nostrils. Hardly a comment falls between us. But I wait . . . musing — in these solemn moments of walking, and talking of melancholia, there's a touch of farce.

You do not draw away from the thorny stalks in your arms, but nose the little red flowers affectionately now and then. She said you were perverse. You are perverse; what is your act? You're talking of painters. I shrug, ignorant. The cultural dimension weaves through your head like the line of an artist who is journeying from edge to edge of her canvas, who pays no attention to destination in filling each moment of space; so much so the line itself is the surprise. Mischief plays in the corners of your face — the dusky light is difficult — no, I see it is intuition: looking at me, reading my thoughts, you say, 'Nature is enough by itself, heh?' But I am thinking of a painter named Burchfield who painted trees like these pines alive with witches — fingers, noses, robes, brooms — troubled by an imminent secrecy. Storms drew Burchfield out into the open with his easel and palette — perhaps this moment poised between two hills, reaching to understand the rosewoman, is the accident for which the odd knowledge of an obscure American artist has been lingering with me for so long.

Witch-non-witch: her first part. Three pubescent girlish voices chanted bubble and trouble. She? Her young eyes lit with the strife she saw through the words into a world on the dark side of the moon — she could not identify it, but the earth became hollow. Stepping gingerly on the mud. A clumsy colour, beyond the perimeter, I, a Banquo not a Macbeth, feel excited by the rising wind and increasing darkness, the moaning heath. The stage is unsuccessfully eerie, veils of mist-gauze fall between the landscape and me: my silly words. She wants to gossip, to pluck at the webs of conflict in the sun-and-housefire world of other humans — I am reluctant to huddle. Either the investigation bores me, or it is not that but a search for bilious discoloured aspects of characters. Towards an agreement, an indictment. I wish to be objective. The land is coming alive with storm. She has forgotten about mud on white plastic as the wind tugs at her nose and knees — surprisingly you mention Thomas Hardy when we stop on the top of a hill facing the west, the strange splash of light there. 'Some sort of sacrificial death on Roman stone,' I answer to the question what happens to Tess in the end. Colours have drained away, we are as black and white as Fate. Two isolations, warm and cold plaiting through us, water and blood. Buffeted by gusts from the south.

When I have milked cows I have loved them, nestled into their warm flanks, spoken soft songs — a country girl who could be happy with dogs and cows and horses and sunshine and gum trees, knee-deep in shit because it is clean — dedicated to the clean and wholesome. These cows we are passing slowly I look at for their blood, for if it were with that I must gain entrance I would slaughter. She withdraws as she climbs the fence. My perception grasps at dribbles in the air, at shades and flickers in the air: woman. The performance is ritual. Loyalty to any past is astonishing, forbidden religion — greening potatoes on the shelf are all that is left of virgin motherhood. She swears and fucks and expels unwanted babes, this other side of woman walking over heathy hills on windy nights. She needs to choose a ritual. The ritual of naturefood for instance, of having cats and a garden full of herbs, of shunning doctors for more mysterious cures; a ritual of calm torment. Of natural perversity. Blood dries on the thorns you hug. A body like yours would choose an English shoe, hesitate at wild flowers asking for the botanical name, plucking leaves for interest in the smell, lending an ear to others' sounds out of that same interest. This radiating curiosity is not a quest of knowledge for a building's sake, nor any logical structure, but a collection, a mass of information to be fascinated by, a storehouse labelled 'mystery'. For worship? woman having no god? Priestess of the no-god-for-women! (Intuition displaces inspiration. And amuses.) You actress! act for me the vampirish tendencies of gentle Sappho, Florence Song-bird's love of wounds, the bloodlust of Joan, the glint in the eye of the Celtic redhead as she is sharpening her knives, visualising them slicing though the thin legs of graceful horses, act out for me the frustration which is in tune with this wind. The gums dance to chaos, the pines whine, an English tree (gold, mistaking winter for autumn) catches our eyes and the last light of evening. Two women stand in the middle of a dirt road looking up at troubled leaves, laughing — we cannot touch, there is an invisible third. We cannot touch in fiction — we both know the severed extremeties of Romance; and the third, the fictional invisible product of our frustration, holds us apart the length of two arms. We are afraid of our possible ritual which may have had something to do with red roses and menstrual blood and knees to the mud, a cackling to match the snapping of branches. Ridiculous.

'Look at that beautiful tree,' you say reverently.

'Don't get me on about English trees in the Australian landscape,' I mumble — piety for piety.

'Oh I'll defend them all — oaks, elms, aspens, holly, poplars.'

A small laugh. 'Chestnuts.'

Sometimes a crazy light dances in your eyes — that mischief: the madness of performing or the performing of madness, I can never tell. With you. Even your tears. And some smiles look so false they might even be sincere — why should I be kind? I want to wring the riddles out of you, to share the irony, or merge it with my earnestness; we stare across an invisible crucifixion of arms. What is love? We cackle, and along a grey stretch of sand mounds hide the bones of those who tried to convince us of love, of oppression. Oh we wanted it, we milked it with such force the teats of its source shrank like a wet plastic bag. He, the trapped oppressor, blushed at the indiscretion of our passion — we sent table-cloths and crockery flying, angered by his inability to give, in revolt against the civilised way he would take — he would be happy to take, he would be tender and affectionate in his taking. We glimpsed the fury beyond give and take. And the glimpse comes back into your eyes.

'Your hands are bleeding,' I say, so sanely.

'I know,' she says, unconcerned, unmoving.

Okay. Handling this living is not so hard, we keep our images under control. So well do we manipulate the slippery emotions day to day we come to our advantage, then ask, 'What is it?' Suddenly the trees are screaming. For us. The torn plant in her arms becomes a bunch of flowers, we look around for the housefire light, see it and sigh. The two of us, near-strangers, with considerate things to say.

'I hope I have not been two-faced.'

'No. I admire your emotional objectivity.'

The storm is outside and will blow over in the night. The wild roses will drop their petals by morning.

Third

Let it be geometry, for instance. The game. Any game. This game. Eyes. We have both realised our art is worthless, one way or another. Eyes, let's say, points on a whole page of blank faces. (The earth is mapped with mine shafts and tunnels — a skeletal emptiness.) The shortest distance between two points is a straight line. One's eye picks and fixes another's, and another's — my interest in these lines as abstract as those on a page of Maths IIA is exploitative. (A mine is invisible from the surface.) A geometrical design of empathy is superimposed on the chaos of crowds.

Now: *let 'eyes' = a, 'yes' = b, 'see' = c.*

$$\frac{abc}{bac} \left(\frac{eyes\ yes\ see}{yes\ eyes\ see} \right) = \frac{Eyes!\ Yes!\ See!}{Yes,\ eyes\ see.}$$

$$\frac{bac}{cba} \left(\frac{yes\ eyes\ see}{see\ yes\ eyes} \right) = \frac{Yes\ —\ eyes\ see.}{See\ yes,\ eyes.}$$

$$\frac{cba}{acb} \left(\frac{see\ yes\ eyes}{eyes\ see\ yes} \right) = \frac{See?\ Yes,\ eyes.}{Eyes\ see\ yes.}$$

$$\frac{acb}{bca} \left(\frac{eyes\ see\ yes}{yes\ see\ eyes} \right) = \frac{Eyes\ see?\ Yes!}{Yes,\ see\ eyes.}$$

$$\frac{bca}{cab} \left(\frac{yes\ see\ eyes}{see\ eyes\ yes} \right) = \frac{Yes\ see;\ eyes.}{See,\ eyes,\ yes.}$$

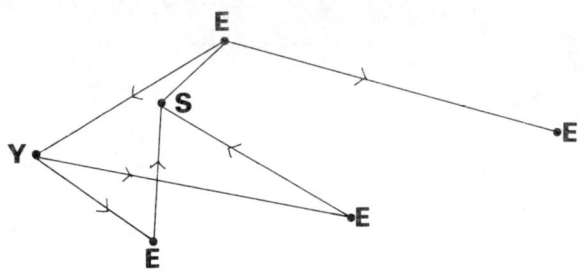

Beneath language are hollow canals, through which we might be sincere in our communication. Affirmation of individuality. I have come to hate the word 'agree' — it attacks my pride. It lacks intuitive/instinctive knowledge. Unless. Unless it came shooting along the channels of empathy . . . as well to be a rose handed through a doorway. A descent through the eye to emptiness, or space. (We mine humour and earnestness, exploring the underground.)

Consider the problem this way, that the empty eyes are questions. Seeking an answer. It does not follow that the blind are lonely, or not lonely. The blind are not alone — the crippled, the poor, the handicapped and complete all can adventure in the invisible, or is it the geometry of possibility? (Data printout: the cautious are most often the survivors.) In human relationships, is it knowledge or illusion that we fear? or conversely, do we fear a map without points and place names? (Theorists attribute the given data to the evidence that the cautious take care of their equipment and allot time to steady work on solid ground before descending. Practitioners argue that it is a matter of the human differential, some survivors are lucky. 'Statistics don't mean a thing when you're down there, swinging your elbows and sniffing soot.' Theorists are anathema to practitioners. Practitioners talk too much, and their talk consists of detail, and useless information it is, involving coincidence, miracles, contradictions, accidents, Acts of God; unforeseen circumstances, the missing appointments, blind loyalty, hunches, moods, the weather.)

Another human being is always a mystery. Words merely attempt wordlessness. Ever studied the science of silence?

The problem has at least the truth of patterns. Emotional patterns born in adolescence, telling feelings to co-ordinate geometry, perhaps. Take the problem of boarding school silence, discipline and shame . . . doodling dreams on a page of Maths IIA. Ultimately learning is the mockery of geometry.

Here is an example of an underground map:

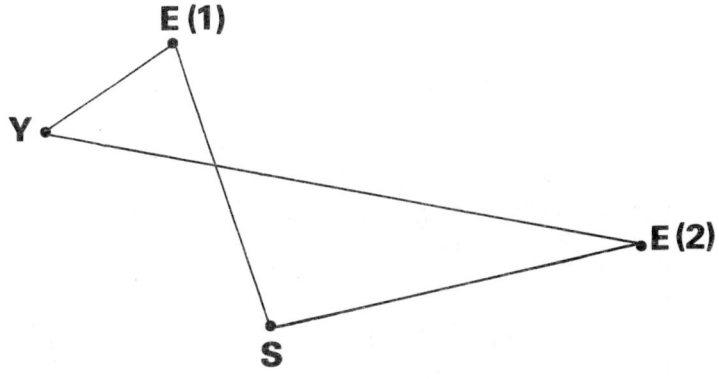

Data: the room has 20 people in it;
  E (1) sits on a couch speaking to x who also sits on the couch;
  E (2) who is leaning in the doorway perceives that E (1) is in fact projecting personality across the room to S;
  S frowns;
  Y provides cigarettes to E (1) casually but readily;
  E (2) catches S's eye, the frown relaxes;
  Y excuses herself, passes a vase of flowers, takes a rose, places it in E (2)'s buttonhole, laughs, and passes through the doorway.

Problem: Y might be an actress who dislikes games, but the room is not a stage.
  Are the seams of a mine created by eye-contact real or fictitious?

Fourth

Members of the public are invited into a den of Dream.

The following litany is transmitted through speakers as audience find their seats in the dark.
Here is the play of light.
Here is the light which does not illuminate.
Here is the reference and the implication.
Here is the play of allusions which illustrate.
Here is the distrust of possibilities.
Here is the crumbling of the wall.
Here is the knowledge that nothing is known.
Here is the mystery.
Here is the contradiction in terms.
Here is the deception and truth, the escape and capture, the fulfilment and frustration.
Here is the elusiveness of reality.
Here is the play: THE ACTRESS IS QUEEN OF ILLUSION.

QUEEN: *(glowing on a pedestal)* I am transparent. You see my soul.

ROSE: *(begging)* If I am a bush give me rain, give me earth for my roots, sun for my flowers, love for my thorns.

RAINDROP: *(dressed as a clown)* If you see a rainbow in me, I am a rainbow.

WORD: *(wearing black skivvy and black jeans)* I speak only of silence.

SCIENCE: *(a parody of Einstein)* If reality equals mystery, nothing that is known is real.

IMAGINATION: *(from the lighting box)* Everything that is known is real.

ROSE: *(searching on the floor)* It is all contained in the dewdrop.

WORD: *(to audience)* Water is transparent.

SCIENCE: The rainbow has no essence in itself, it is only light and water.

QUEEN: *(becoming discomforted)* Colours we know — don't you see?

(RAINDROP *bounds up to the pedestal in response to a gesture from* QUEEN.)
RAINDROP AND QUEEN: *(together)* We are transparent, but it's colours we know, don't you see?
IMAGINATION: *(helpfully)* I see us all within the huge transparent sphere of mystery.
WORD: *(confidently, pacing across stage front)* If I am a bush give me air and moisture, earth and sun! *(mildly amused)* Let me explain: take, for example, this bush. The roots, you see, are Latin through French, 'ludere lus'; originally meaning 'play', the flowers, this season, are 'allusion', 'elusiveness' and 'illusion'. The bush is real, the roots, the leaves, the thorns all real, adding up to deception. All I can ever do is play the game of deception.
(Unscripted movement breaks out on stage)
SCIENCE: I disagree.
IMAGINATION: So do I.
ROSE: The trouble with you, Word, is that you try to be more than you are.
QUEEN: *(trying to redeem situation)* A rose is a rose is a rose is . . .
MEMBER OF THE AUDIENCE: What a boring show!
(troubled whispering among performers)
QUEEN: What we need is . . .
IMAGINATION: *(interrupting)* Physicalisation.
QUEEN: *(physicalising)* The real rose!
WORD: *(turning to Rose)* I know! I'll crawl out of your mouth.
ROSE: *(indignantly)* You will not!
SCIENCE: That's false, a rose doesn't talk.
RAINDROP: *(doing a somersault)* What a mess!
MEMBER OF THE AUDIENCE: *(amid the deafening sound of seats slapping)* This is a rip-off.
(THE WRITER *leaps up from the darkest corner in the back row*)
WRITER: *(fighting her way down the aisle)* You're all fucking corrupt! You won't even give me time to try. Let me through. It's all a matter of light . . .
BLACKOUT. SILENCE. *(A huge crash is heard.* IMAGINATION *has fallen out of the lighting box.)*

Fifth

Don't worry, no one will recognise you. The game is fiction. You do not exist. I became so in love with you that I wondered whether in fact I existed: at times I did not exist. Instead of me there was you. I did not know myself, I was an alienated soul — a disembodied flight of the imagination — heroine of the dream. I made a stage, the sets were dangerously insecure. I tripped, the finger holes of my gloves were sewn up. I continued, handicapped . . . Chasing you down the dusk, and into the storm. It was not, it is not the illusive quality of the actual things, rather the actual quality of illusive things. The style creates reality — is that it? If they look they will find your name, and fuel for their slanderous fires. They may even love you — you do not exist. You are safe. I am not guilty of theft. From you. Of you. The second person pronoun is the possession of anybody, anybody at all, with words in their hands. You do not say of course, you question and you question until you've pushed away all the layers of earth and found that rock becomes boiling liquid. Reality to you is fiery then, and untouchable, is it? I came around on a misty Saturday to ask you — is it? You were again, elusive. I needed something solid, something real from the mirage — a spot of rose-hip tea on the page, anything; a thorn? Words, yes, words to place between inverted commas and say you said them . . . Whatever you said you contradicted soon afterwards. Your contradictions bind me . . . give me daydreams full of abundance . . . daydreams that feed on the impossible and fester, and spread like fungus. Behind this performance and the next performance and the next performance, where is the emptiness? But you play constantly, shadows on the wall of your cave . . . dance murder mystery irony chill and warmth . . . (if the church and the theatre had the same roots, and man and woman the same roots too, then the church is masculine and the theatre feminine — the thought merely occurs to me). Here's the twist, you were nothing but a well of reflections and it was I who walked across the heathy hills, wind blowing a veil of thin gauze across my face. Thinking of witchery. I who read what I chose to in your eyes. I who created a love for myself ... I who let my emotions range over a whole spectrum of impossibilities. Even so, it was love. Or, a —simulacrum?

Appendix

'Confession From A Ghost-White Skin', from 'Three Panels Of Prose', *Màkar*, Vol 11, No 3, December, 1976
'So, Sandra', *Aspect*, February, 1976
'Five Finger Exercises', *New Poetry*, Vol 25, No 2, 1975
'Conversation Without Inverted Commas', *Westerly*, No 1, March, 1977
'Jillian Arbus', *Meanjin*, April, 1976
'Seven Abortions', *Westerly*, No 1, March, 1975
'Bloomsbury's Son', *Comtempa*, 10, 1973
'Moreton Bay Fig', as part of 'Three Pieces From Middle Class Novel', *Meanjin*, February, 1978
'Goodbye Prince Hamlet: the New Australian Women's Poetry', an extract from a review with the same title, *Meanjin*, February, 1975
'Screams From A Primal Quarter', *Mother I'm Rooted*, Kate Jennings (ed), Outback Press, Melbourne, 1975
'Bella', ibid
'Prose Looks At Photographs', *Luna*, No 1, 1975
'The Room With A Mirror', from 'The Three Panels Of Prose', op cit
'Where Are You, Ellen Spalding', *Refractory Girl*, No 10, March, 1976
'The Rubbish Tin Outside Federation Café', *Southerly*, No 2, 1975
'Who Cares About The Sentence?', *Journal From The Paper Castle*, 1974
'Nun', *Frictions*, Anna Gibbs and Alison Tilson (eds), Sybylla Press, Melbourne, 1982
'Happening Upon A Character, In The First Person', from 'Three Pieces From Middle Class Novel', op cit
'A Bit Of The Learning Bit', ibid
'Novel In Ten Lines', *Frictions*, op cit
'The Illusive Quality Stories', *Meanjin*, April, 1975